I did not think about it.
I put on his shirt and stood in front of him, as if to make him understand that I want his smell on him.
I mentally slap myself, but at the same time I don't understand why he gets so angry because I put on his shirt.
Silence dominates the hall: what could I answer him?
«I thought it was mine!» - I spit the first thing that comes to my mind, but he doesn't stop looking me straight in the eyes with those dark puddles in which I seem to be about to drown.
His breathing is mixed with mine and I would really like to move away, but my feet are nailed to the floor against my will.
I look away for a moment, but immediately after they return to his and I use every single cell of my body so as not to get closer to him at this moment.
«Sure.» - he laughs bitterly, then looks away and brings him down, towards my legs. I feel completely naked before her eyes, but the first promise I make to myself is not to allow him to possess me anymore.
For me from now on he will be only a stranger, even if he doesn't want to leave and we would be forced to live under one roof.

I take this opportunity to look nostalgic at every inch of skin uncovered on his neck and stained with tattoos, while his

hand crosses the border that I had mentally established between our bodies, to grasp the edge of the shirt between two fingers.
In doing so he does not look at me, but accidentally touches my skin under the fabric, whereupon I suddenly move away from him.
Because it's a magnet, that's what Alex is, a magnet capable of dragging only trouble and women ...

I felt love for him and I was not reciprocated, but I will not continue to drool after him.

He still doesn't look at me, but his expression says everything except calm and sadness, I don't want to know what is whipping in his head, so I remain silent, almost waiting for him to tell me something, while he turns his back on me carrying a hand between hair, and then go to the sofa. A strong man, proud and self-confident, that's what I find myself in front of, but above all, a lonely man who doesn't know what he wants ...

«Catherine is gone. You can sleep in peace. »- he says in a resigned voice, reminding me to find myself still in the middle of the living room staring at him.

On the contrary, I don't answer, I go back slowly in the bedroom, throwing myself on the giant bed like a sack of potatoes.
I even forget to cover myself for the very unattractive thoughts invade my head, while I let myself be embraced by Morpheus clutching me in Alex's shirt.

I feel myself shaking my shoulder, while, listless, I try to give an answer to complete sense, not even taking into account what I say.
«But I'm not Alex, I'm Juliet. If you don't accompany me to school I will make a terrible delay and Professor Louis will kill me ! »- she says alarmed, so I try to open one eye after

another, realizing only now that Juliet is sitting astride on my
back.
That's why I felt I had a boulder on my shoulders and I
dreamed of having ended up among the proud of Dante's
purgatory.
«Forget it, let your brother accompany you !» - I
say trying to go back to sleep. "He's not home." -
his answer makes me open my eyes again.
I look at the clock hanging on the wall: it's
seven in the morning, where will it have ended
at this hour? I roll my eyes, the answer to my
question is obvious ...
«Move, I have to change.» - I snort, while I think of the worst
that could happen in taking her to school: meet Louis.
«Next year I will sign you up and take the bus.» - I say, as I
hurry to change, but then I realize that she is ready, then I
narrow my eyes, glancing again at the clock.
"Wait ... it's only seven o'clock, you'd be half an hour
early even if you walked alone." He shrugs and takes
on a sweet but premonitory expression of trouble.
"Uffà? Eh okay, I have to meet with Cameron! »- jumps
around the place, while I open my mouth.

"Juliet! Your brother would kill me if he found out. "
"At best he would get a little angry, but he will never find out,
promise!" - he replies, trying to convince me.
«I promise you!» - he adds, making me puff, while I change
the shirt, putting it back in the special drawer.

I follow her out of the entrance, without forgetting my purse
and phone, so that I can go straight to work.
"You know I don't want to meet Louis these days, Juliet!" - I
continue to complain in vain, as we are already driving
towards school.
"Sooner or later you will see each other again." - he adds
casually.

«Better then than before.» - I whisper to myself, while the girl turns her head out the window.

«Here we are, you can get off here!» - I stop the car ten meters away from the entrance, while she rolls her eyes, slamming the door behind her.
«Good school!» - I scream a few seconds later, then I hurry away from the building, reversing.
I slow down, as soon as I notice the hospital structure from afar and pray to find a free parking space.
After three quarters of an hour of research, I finally put the car in an empty place, most likely the last one left.
As soon as I am inside the hospital I think about the fact that I will finally be able to get away from all the problems of my private life.

But it still seems too early to go inside, so without thinking twice, I pick up the phone to call my friend.
But he seems to read me in thought and anticipates me, in fact, when I open the phone book to look for his name, the phone marks the arrival of a message from John asking to meet him as soon as possible.

Hoping that nothing serious had happened and that it was just one of his usual exaggerations, I replied to him to come to the canteen of the right wing of the hospital.
I cross the front door, while the scene of every morning appears before me: there are those who run, including many nurses, those who are half asleep on the armchairs of the gigantic waiting room, others, however, look around as if it was the first time they set foot in this hospital.
When I was hired, especially the first few days, I stopped to

look at the expressions of everyone present in this room to

understand their stories, but I stopped doing it after about a year, when the work started to be more intense and when I

started to get tired so much I fell asleep on my feet rather

than staring at patients.

I smile mentally remembering the first night shift, but then I
started to get used to all the mess going on in here, a mess
and movement not even found in a disco.
Getting lost in thoughts, I start to walk towards my goal, but I
am blocked by a hand that rests on my shoulder.
I turn around quickly, but I relax when I notice that he is the
primary, as well as Louis's father, Catherine's father, and the
one who saw me beat his daughter.
But, unlike what I would have expected, his gaze is that of an
understanding man and not a boss who would be about to fire
someone.
"My son said you wanted to talk to me." - he says, and I hope
his son just told him that. I nodded slowly, then opened my
mouth:
«Yes, yes, but it doesn't seem the right place to me .» - I look
around, but interrupts me.
"If it's because of the fight between you and my daughter, I'm
going to have to apologize. It's not the first time my daughter
gets into trouble, and if she even managed to infuriate you, it
means she's done it big. "
I lower my head to his words: he did it big, yes!
"But she's the one who has to apologize in person, that's why I
wanted to invite you to a dinner at my house. You and my
family. What do you say?"
I immediately shake my head, but knowing him he won't give
up easily.
«Come on, daughter, I also want to take advantage of
knowing better the future manager of our department.» - he
winks at me smiling.

«It depends on the day, lately I am very busy ...» - I try to sneak away, but his answer is immediate:
"I won't be there in these two weeks, so for the Thursday of the week after get rid of all your commitments." - he replies, and then leaves the structure.
I snort, rolling my eyes: I don't know what is worse, the fact that I will have to see Louis again, which I thought I would avoid all my life, or the fact that I will be sitting in front of Catherine around the same table.

I resign myself, reaching the bar, where I already find my friend with his arms crossed and with a frown on his face. "I've been waiting for ten minutes !" - he pouts.
«He is talking about someone who does not even know what punctuality is.» - I embrace him from the shoulders, pressing his lips against his cheek.
"We two have to talk!" - the tone of his voice says so much, like the subject of the discussion is me.
"Can we stay silent until eight o'clock instead?" - I take a seat and order a coffee from the barista, while my friend does not deprive himself of that severe expression.
"Why didn't you tell
me that you and Alex
broke up?" His
words hit me in the
face: did we break
up?
Hearing it hurts so badly that I would have preferred a slap instead of these words. "Who-who you did it say?" - He furrowed his eyebrows, while I bite the inside of his cheek to keep from crying in front of him.
"Many have told me, Tiara, Andrew ... But does it matter what?" - I lower my head, staring at the cup of coffee, the smell of which invades my nostrils:
"Are you okay?" - because everyone has to ask me this question if in the end they already know the answer.

If Andrew told him that, it means he spoke to Alex about it,
and it was Alex who told him it's over between us. So we
broke up for him? He didn't even commit himself to trying to
put things right.

«It's already eight o'clock, I have to go!» - I pretend a serene
expression, and then run away leaving the coffee on the
counter and my friend curious to know what it is that I don't
have the courage to talk about.
But I'm not going to shed an extra tear for Alex, so at a
leisurely pace I head for the first patient.

As soon as I reach the room I notice that the woman is not alone, but in the
company of her husband.
I stop at my steps, to watch them holding hands from the
outside of room 32 on the first floor. I tilt my head and get
lost in that scene, seeing myself in its place, but immediately
I chase my thoughts away when I am dragged to reality by
my phone:
"Mum? What's up? I'm working. "- I inform her, but she neglects my words,
to speak to me above:
"You're going back to America!" - I hear her screaming
across the line. I open my eyes as my heart starts to beat
so hard that it seems to want to get out of the place

She has never been so angry,
so she must have serious
reasons. "Why? Did
something happen? Is Dad
okay? "
«You will not live alone in such a big city! Will you be home
by next Monday, or will I be the one who will drag you here!
»- I open my mouth, not knowing what to say.

"Mom, are you going crazy, by any chance? Pass me dad! »- it really starts to frighten me his authoritarian tone. "It would be better for you that your father found out about you and not me!" "What do you need to know?" - impatient snort .
"That you and Alex broke up! Here's what! And I find out from Clelia, of course, because my daughter is too busy to call her mother and tell her that she lives alone in Australia while Alex spends the nights who knows where and with whom! The Australian dream is over and in five days I want you in America! "

His words leave me perplexed and disappointed, first of all because I am of an age to acquire a certain independence from my parents, but also because my mother knew, surely because of Tiara, that this is a difficult period for me, but it doesn't he doesn't even try to console me, on the contrary, he shamelessly requires me to move to America.

Knowing her, though, if I told her all this, it would be neither hot nor cold, but I can't risk losing everything because of Alex: «Mom, Alex and I only made a joke on Tiara ...» - I try to be as convincing as possible, but immediately I hear her reply:
"Joke?! What kind of jokes are these, huh ?! "
«Tiara was making fun of us, so ... whatever it is, don't worry, even on my own I could take care of myself. That's what I did even when I lived in Italy. "- I remember them.
'You were there anyway with your aunt. However, I am not convinced by your tone of voice. »- she seems to be saying it more to herself than to me.
"I'm tired and I'm about to have a transplant, Mom, what tone of voice would you expect to hear?" He just sighs, a sign of the fact that he is making dangerous thoughts, so I say goodbye and, without waiting for his reply, I close the call.

I head to the operating room, ready for three hours of intense work and maximum attention, which for me means rest and alienation from reality.

I arrive in front of the sink wearing a pair of gloves, while the smell of latex pokes my nostrils, and sterilizing them.
I work alongside my colleague and the nurses who will help me with this intervention, while the doors close and the lights become more concentrated.
Only on these occasions do I feel that it was really worth it to spend ten years of study and isolation, and only in moments like this I feel ... useful.
Saving a person's life is the best way to do charity and to feel fulfilled.

I really want my job to be enough to forget my private life: I could lock myself in this room for days and continue doing difficult operations to patients with chronic diseases, just to get Alex out of my head, but I know it would be useless.
I have always feared this strong feeling towards him, as if I knew that one day I would suffer from it without being able to do anything to get out of it.

As soon as I finish sewing the last piece of leather after hours that have seemed centuries, I feel my hands tremble, while my legs can't stand anymore.
I suddenly fall to the ground as my eyes plunge into total darkness.

C
h
a
p
t
e
r

2
5

Alex

"Give her some more time, let her breathe." - Andrew tries to convince me as I throw another punch in the sack in front of me.

"I gave her enough time !" - I say frankly and pissed.

«You still have to get used to the fact that you and Catherine are friends.» - he says calmly, but does not know that I am going crazy right now because of that brat.

«I can't wait, Andrew ...» - and I'm dying to see her laughing again, I would like to add, but I just snort and let off steam with the boulder in front of me.

The jerk in front of me suggested that I stay calm and 'give her some time', but it is already a lot if I didn't rap her on her feet last night when I saw her with her bare legs.

By the way, it hasn't worked so far ...

And then Catherine continues to seem like a justification: she can't be pissed at me just because I have a female being as a friend.

«I understand that your cock is bursting in your underwear, but think before doing some shit. Clara is a delicate girl . »- she says obviously, while I look down between the legs.

But not only do I feel the desire to touch her, it would be enough for me to see her sleeping beside me, to wake up with her head to the hollow of my neck. In fact, lately I realized how uncomfortable our sofa is.

She is a delicate girl ...

She doesn't seem so delicate when she gets jealous, since she even punched Catherine. When she came to tell me, complaining of the bruises, at first I could not hold back the laughter, thinking of Clara jumping on her for me, but then I understood that this meant many things. Like Clara isn't kidding and, if it got to her hands, the matter is more serious for her than it is for me.

"How much longer do I have to wait?"

C
h
a
p
t
e
r

2
6

I've always loved the smell of latex, but right now it's so strong that I force myself to slowly open my eyes.
I close it again when I am struck by the dazzling light of the room where I am.

I frown when, even if after a long time, I realize that I am in a hospital room, and not in the clothes of the doctor, but of the patient.
I try to remember what happened, frowning, but the last episode that comes back to me is the intervention of Katty Mail.

I try to turn my neck, but a sharp twinge of pain runs through the top of my spine.

"Ah, you've recovered!" - John's voice fills the room and I'm glad of his presence in this moment of confusion.
As she brings her head before my eyes, I
ask him to help me go back to sitting.
«Careful ...» - she looks at me sideways, almost perplexed.

«What happened?» - I ask slowly, while I put a hand on my forehead, imagining how beautiful a bruise can be evident in the part that I try to touch and that really hurts.

«Don't you remember?» - continues to give me that annoying look, but I just shrug my shoulders and wait for an answer, in vain, because a nurse enters.

«Doctor, I'm sorry, I hope you get well soon.» - she smiles, while I mentally curse myself for not recognizing her: if she gives me that smile it means that most likely we have also worked together, but I don't remember her face. I slowly nod: «I'm fine, I only have a very strong headache. I fell? What happened to me? "

«You are passed out.» - my friend scratches the back of his neck, raising one corner of his mouth, while the nurse takes the floor again:

"But he only hit his head, luckily the beans are healthy." - she says cheerfully.

I snap my head up:
"Green beans?" - I assume a frowning expression, while my friend hurries to put his hand on the woman's back, moving her away from the room and quickly closing the door.

«Clara ...» - begins to approach, but, with a terrified expression, I look towards the belly: "Thing? What did you mean, John ... »- I try to stand up, but I give up after several attempts in which the pain takes over.

"Take it easy! Come back ... »- I wo n't let him finish that I give voice to my thoughts: "I can't be pregnant, there can't be a baby in here!" - I hope it disproves everything, while my eyes are clouded with tears.

"In fact, you don't have a baby." - I open my eyes, starting to calm down and start breathing again. «You have two.» - he smiles innocently.

I feel my hands tremble as I bring them closer to my belly,
then immediately move them away and look away. "I have
two of them?"
"And they're as healthy as a fish, you could have risked for anesthetic
gases, Clara. You could have hurt them. "

«Could I hurt them ?» - I keep repeating his words like an
idiot, while a strange and never felt sensation overwhelms me.

«Hey, calm down ... look me in the eyes.» - urges me to raise
my head, while my eyes continue to be clouded by tears, which
seem frozen and do not want to go down. I look at him stunned,
while John tries to give me a reassuring smile.

«It's a beautiful thing, small, and you know it better than me.»
- I swallow the lump in my throat, but even if I mentally repeat
his words I can't convince myself.
How could it be beautiful?
«I'm not ready to become a mother.» - I spit in a broken voice,
even having difficulty formulating a sentence.
«There is no need to prepare. These twins will bring so many beautiful
things, don't think about obstacles. "

Instead in my head I think only of the worst, the fact that I
will be away from my job for a long time, the fact that
everyone would know it, but above all problems ... there is
Alex.

I'm expecting two children from him: right now that I don't
even want to see his face, I find that two miniature 'Alexs'
grow in my belly.
I will be forced to find myself in front, most likely, the same
eyes and the same bullshit all my life.
Unless...

I've always been against abortion, I've always
considered it a crime to avoid. But now I find
myself in a frightening position.
After all ... this is the biggest problem: I'm afraid.
I would never be able to overcome such a big obstacle alone. I
would not be able to face my mother and all those who
discover sooner or later that Alex and I are finished, I would
not be able to sleep with the idea that two living beings grow
in me that I will have to look after and I would never be able to
look at Alex in the eyes to tell him I'm pregnant with him.
«How many weeks are they?» - I hasten to ask in a cold tone
and dispelling the tears.
"Almost two months, and don't even think about it!"
«I ca n't ...» - I begin to motivate my decision, but it doesn't
even give me time to release the tears that his hand grasps my
wrist, while with the other he raises my shirt, uncovering his
belly.
«What are you doing?!» - my voice comes out in a strangled
scream and I try to free myself from his grip, but he drags my
hand on the bare skin, pressing lightly on it.
«Leave me!» - I reply, while under the palm of my hand I
perceive slight movements.
At that point I notice the tears that reach my chin, while John
loosens his grip around my wrist, looking at me with
compassion.

I remain motionless, concentrating on every single kick of my
twins, almost wanting to communicate with them.

For a moment I forget John's presence and the hospital,
getting lost in my thoughts again

I'm pregnant. I raise one corner of my
mouth upwards, giving voice to my
thoughts: «I am pregnant!» - I exclaim in
front of John who imitates me, showing a
big smile. He greets me on the neck,

anticipating me, while I take a deep
breath.

I really thought about depriving myself of something that is
mine only because of the people around me, and just for
considering it among the possible options I mentally throw so
many slaps to pass out.

I didn't know I was pregnant, but now I understand the reason
for my vomiting and the fact that lately I feel very tired in the
morning.

If only something had happened in the operating room,
besides a simple fainting, I would never have forgiven myself.

Time goes by without my noticing it, as I continue to
stare at the slightly swollen belly like a sling.
"Honestly, I thought you were gaining weight lately, by the
belly, I mean ..." - his eyes focus on the same point where
mine end up again.
I laugh at his words.
I laugh to relieve myself of all the stress I have had to endure
lately and not because his words amuse me.

It won't be that bad.
Strange how things sometimes go: there are women who do everything to
have a child, but they cannot
and are forced to adopt one, like my mother, and others who,
instead, do everything to get rid of it. I never stopped to
judge, because I never knew what it meant to be a mother.

I was furious when I learned that I had been adopted, both with
my biological and adoptive parents, I didn't even bother to put

myself in their shoes. I have never seen myself in the guise of a parent.

And now?
My belly will get bigger and bigger and I won't be able to hide the evidence. But how do you tell others? How would they take it?

Alex ...
Alex will be the father of my children.

In my head I think of how to tell him: it would not be a novelty for him, being already a father, but Tiara told me that he didn't take it very well, so much so that he forced Naily to bring Giulietta to the orphanage

Now things have changed,
but I don't trust Alex for
obvious reasons. " You tell
her?" - I remember John's
presence for his words. I
close my eyes and without
even thinking about it, I
answer immediately:

«Of course!» - I would never be able to hide it from him, and I couldn't, since at some point I will find myself a belly that is impossible to cover.
I really want to make him feel bad about how he treated me, but not like this ...

I do not know what reaction to expect from him: I have always dreamed of such a moment, imagining to tell him by surprise, also because I wanted to start a family with him.

But he doesn't ...

«You would do the right thing .» - he indulges me with a little
delay, and then helps me to better position the cushions
behind me.
I nod, continuing to think about how to report this to him,
without slapping him for his attitude.

I trace imaginary circles around the navel as I reflect on their
future.
I already feel guilty for not being able to give them a nice
united family, while I imagine what it will be like to live with two
nuisances around the house.
I have already had this experience in part with Giulietta, but she is very
independent and does not disturb.

"How are you
feeling?" - John
looks at me
intently. "I do
n't know.," - I
admit.
In fact, a mixture of feelings is really confusing my ideas.
It is true that I wanted a family, but then
I always put off my dreams. I am angry,
sad and regretful because my
children's father is an asshole. But I'm
also ... happy.
So much so that I would like to communicate this good news
to all those around me, although I would not receive the
reaction I am hoping for from anyone.

"Who knows what they are thinking right now." - my friend
fearfully rests his hand on my belly.

«They don't have a brain.» - I continue to caress my belly,
as if in its place there was the head of one of the 'green
beans', admiring the belly as if I were in front of a magical
creature. "Then they took it from their father." - he says, only
to stop when it's too late now, but all I do is raise a corner of
my mouth.

I will never get used to the idea of having 'green beans'
growing in my belly.

I jerk my head up, suddenly freeing myself of all thoughts
concerning my parents, Alex and Catherine:
"There is a problem."
«What 's up?!» - opens his eyes wide worried, standing up.
"I need advice, books, magazines! Anything that talks about pregnancy! »-
he sighs rolling his eyes.
"All right. I'll take you to a bookstore later. But you don't need
a mom magazine to understand that you need to take days off
immediately.
So, before leaving we go to ... »- begins, but is interrupted by
the figure of the primary who makes his entrance with his son.
I wonder why Louis was there if he has to be at school
teaching Juliet at this hour. It embarrasses me despite the
situation I'm in.
I don't want her to know I'm pregnant, but I don't know why.
The sure thing is that we could never be friends as
before: after the kiss, things between us have changed
drastically.
I lower my eyes as I try to formulate an answer to the doctor's
question:
"Clara? I heard you were passed out. Everything good?"
But the words get stuck in my throat, so my best friend
intervenes, turning to Louis who keeps looking at me
insistently:
«Leave them alone.» - he says gently, stroking my hair, while I
thank him mentally, keeping my eyes on the floor until the
moment I hear the door slam and close.

For a moment I had forgotten about the job. I did a lot to get
here, I really gave up adolescence and fun, and it's bad to
erase everything in the blink of an eye.
Giving up on one of the things I'm proud of isn't so simple,
but only now do I notice it. I should have thought about it,
thinking about having a family isn't child's play, it's not
about sitting on a chair and spending the days on
university books.
I don't know how much I will endure staying at home without doing anything,
without even visiting a patient. But I don't even think about continuing to
work, even if it does not imply interventions in operating theaters.

«I don't know how to ask him ...» - I say in a low voice.
Infondo is one of the people who trusted me most from the first day I
set foot in this hospital and who expects a lot from me.
He even said he wanted to leave me his post, even if it
doesn't entirely depend on him. And I've never been
afraid to take responsibility for an entire hospital ward,
but raising two kids is already freaking me out.

"Is it a serious problem? What do the
analyzes say ? »- he asks regardless of my
embarrassment. I shake my head.
«But I need days off.» - I raise my
head, looking him in the eyes.
"Sure! How many? »- approaches
the head of the bed with a padded
foot.
"Ten months."

Chapter

27

Alex

I squeeze the glass between my fingers, while my breasts turn white.
I keep staring at the door in front of me, almost waiting for it to come in at any moment. I look again at the clock on the wall that says one in the morning.
I run my fingers through my hair, then slam a fist into the frustrated table.

I don't know where she is at this hour, but in my fucking head I imagine Clara and that fucking teacher together.

I get up and walk around the hall in a plush pace, addressing
the person you most hate:

Catherine ...

C
h
a
p
t
e
r

2
8

«Why are you buying pink shirts? You don't know if they are
both female. "

As soon as I got out of the hospital, although it was midnight, I
asked John to accompany me to a baby clothes shop.
Strangely, he did not oppose or take for mad, but simply got
up and helped me walk the corridors of the hospital.

I shrug my question.
"I've always wanted a first daughter ..."
Raise your eyes to the sky, while I look at
the outfits hanging with tears in my eyes. I
hear my friend walking away for a
moment, walking around the shop:
«If Tiara and Jessica were here they would give you reason.»
- she continues to scream, despite the saleswoman
continuing to glare at us for the fact that we literally
threatened her not to close on time.

"If only Tiara knew ..." - I repeat to myself.

I am slightly angry with her, for telling my father that things are not going great between me and Alex, but all in all I expected it.
And I would also like not to have to lie to my mother, I would like to inform her first that she will become a grandmother twice, but I can't. At least for now.
«Don't talk to anyone, please.» - I say, aloud. «Why?» - he asks distractedly, picking up a yellow suit.

Because? Because I'm afraid of their answer: my father insisted so much on a marriage between me and Alex, and I don't know how such news would take her. Not to mention my mother, who would be able to trigger an uproar.

«Alex will be waiting for you.» - he says all of a sudden, pretending a neutral tone of voice. "Alex will stay with Catherine." - I reply , of course.
"Are you going to tell her tonight?" - he asks.
«I don't think I'll find him at home.» - I just answer.

I think about what she is thinking right now, or where she is, and I hate to admit it, but I think Catherine is leaving traces on her body right now.
I squeeze my jaw, trying again to drive away from the head Maybe he will get angry when he finds out: who knows what he will feel in being a father for a second time. "How do you think he's going to take it?" - John seems to read my thoughts, but I can't answer his questions.

"I do not know. Maybe he'll abandon me like he did with Naily.
"- my voice only trembles when I
say those words.
John doesn't answer, almost wanting to agree with my
reasoning, which really hurts.
It means I'm not the only one who understands that Alex
doesn't care about me. Sometimes I lie to myself and I
delude myself that all this is the result of my imagination,
that Alex ...
continues to love me. Or who thinks of me as I think of him.
Just the idea that we are now sharing two children makes me
hope that things will change. But I can never look at it the
same way, I can never imagine her skin on mine after
Catherine touched her.

«I'll help you .» - she takes the envelopes out of my hand,
before she can even leave the shop.
"I'm just pregnant ..." - I roll my eyes, smiling, while he
anticipates me entering the car.

"Thanks. Really. »- I look him
in the eye and he gives me a
wink. He is a great friend and
I am happy to have at least
his support.

If he wasn't there, I wouldn't be able to talk to anyone about
my problems and my private life. He accompanied me and
he was close to me in a moment like this, in which I don't
feel like anything: he didn't think twice before, in fact, before
settle and accompany me to buy clothes for the twins.

As soon as we find ourselves in front of the blue painted door I
stop breathing and go looking for Alex's car in the courtyard.
I find it parked next to the rose plants, so I take a deep breath.

It is more difficult than I thought: I fear his answer, I fear that he says something that I will not like to hear and I prepare myself for the worst.
But the things between the two of us couldn't be worse than they are.
Mentally I think about how I would have taken the news of being pregnant if I had never found out about Catherine and Alex.
Surely I would have burst into tears of joy and I would not have thought of abandoning my children in an orphanage, then I would have run to tell him instead of going to a shop immediately after the great discovery. I would have kissed him and seen in him the future father of two babies in his arms.
While my gaze is lost outside the window and ends up on the rusty rocking chair in front of the entrance, the image of Alex filling the babies with kisses appears before my eyes.

He wears a sweatshirt that I then steal from him before bed to fall asleep with his perfume on him, even though there is one I have two centimeters away by my side on the bed. Then he makes me spend an unforgettable night, making me try new things never tried before. But then we are interrupted by one of the little ones who cries, so Alex complains and says that it's up to me to go and change them. I snort, leaving him naked on the bed ...

«If you want we can spend the rest of the night here, but tomorrow I have to work.» - I jump at the voice of John who puts his arm on the steering wheel, careful not to honk.
"I'm sorry for you." - I shrug.
«Yes, at this point I would also like to have a green bean inside my belly.» - I laugh forcefully, while leaving my place.

He goes down to open the trunk, so I grab everything I
bought for a quarter of my salary. I greet him with a kiss
on the cheek, while he glances at me to encourage me.
«You are doing the right thing .» - puts a hand on my shoulder
and then leaves a kiss on my hair. I nod confidently.
Telling him to expect Alex's worst insults would be better than
keeping it hidden from him.

With a trembling hand, I take the key from one of the countless
envelopes that I hold, then insert the key in the keyhole of the
main door, and then cross the threshold at the exact moment
when John's car whizzes away.
The dazzling light of the living room demoralizes me because
it is an indication that Alex is not only at home, but is also
awake.

Maybe for a moment I was hoping I could postpone our
conversation the next day, but luck is never on my side.

I look up from the floor, startled in fright when I see him with
his arms crossed leaning against a column, while his eyes
stare at me carefully.
I would like to look away from his hypnotist, while the words
get stuck in the throat: it is impossible to look him in the eye to
tell him that ... he will become a dad.
He is angry, he is seen by the swollen vein in relief that starts
from the root of his neck and reaches the height of the jaw.
It is the anger of a man who despises me and
who is ready to show his claws: «We have to
talk.» - my voice comes out less sure than I would
have liked, but he interrupts me, approaching the
door.
I swallow the lump in my throat, fearing every single step,
especially when I notice the bloodshot eyes from afar.

He drank.

I feel the stench of alcohol replacing its true scent, so I
grimace.
When I find him almost three steps away I step back on my
own, finding myself stuck against the door, but he too stops.
He stops, continuing to look at me from head to toe with an
indescribable expression, but then bursts out laughing, leaving
me perplexed.
«You have avoided me for days and now you want to talk to me.» - he
analyzes, continuing to laugh bitterly.

She seems lucid enough to face a speech and not do or
say things she forgets the next day, so I retort, suddenly
angry:
«For obvious reasons .» - I try to look at him with the
same intensity with which his eyes pierce me, but my
expression turns into a grimace when I notice red marks
on his neck. I open my eyes and then immediately lower
my head, trying not to think about what he has done so
far.

I wear a strand of hair behind my ear in frustration, while he
continues to prick me:
«What is it?» - you touch the point where my eyes were
pointed with the thumb, raising a corner of the mouth: « Does
it bother you?» - he gets even closer, while the strong smell of
alcohol strikes my nostrils.
I tilt my head and with all my strength I drive away the tears
that start to hinder my vision. I squeeze the envelopes
between my fingers, while he takes my chin between the
thumb and forefinger and forces me to look up, immersing
myself in his darker puddles than usual.

It is not the first time that I see him in this state, but his words
come straight to my soul and hurt more than his bad looks.

My eyes go from hers to her neck, dirty from another woman's
lips.

A tear falls without my being able to control it, even though
everything I feel for him at the moment is pure crap, but this
does not seem to have any effect on him:
"You can do whatever you want with whoever you want, as you always
have." - clamps his jaw to my words.
«I was at Catherine's.» - she says looking at me as if she
wanted to study my reaction, but I really knew it. On the other
hand, hearing him admit it destroys me:
« Shut up.» - I say almost pleading, but the tone of my voice
seems to encourage him to continue to hurt me.
«I was at his house .» - he sighs on my face, almost
wanting to hurt me with his breath. « Shut up.» - I keep
pleading with him, this time more determined than
before, but he doesn't remove that damned smile from
his face and his dimples annoy me for the first time.
"In his room..."
«Shut up ...» - pleading sob , while I slide against the door at
the bottom, without leaving the envelopes on the ground.
She does not lower herself to my height, but returns to torment
me and make me find myself in front of every moment lived
with her.

I hate him, I despise him even more than before.

«I fucked her ...» - I snap my head upwards, finding myself
in front of a stranger and, without letting him continue, I go
over him in a fleecy step and arrive in my room.
In what used to be our room.
My blurred eyes immediately end up on the bed where we
spent the most beautiful and exciting nights together.
I look at him with nostalgia, trying to remember every single
kiss, every single caress on his part, then I think how much
these moments were false, futile, spent with the wrong person
...

Because Alex will never be the man I loved, and he never was.

I was blind, but now I find myself in front of the real Alex, the asshole bitch who never reciprocated me. If he had really wanted me, or if he had at least tried something for me, he would never have had the courage to look me straight in the eye and spit the truth at me, but he wouldn't even have entered another woman's underwear.

I will not need and have mercy on him, as he did not think of me.

Now everything is clear, it was fun for him to make fun of a woman all over the house and the Church, but now he got tired of all my naivety and went hunting for expert women. I'm not even comparable to someone like Catherine, because I'm not sexy like her, I can't treat her body like she apparently can. I am not enough for him.

«I hate you ...» - I whisper to myself, looking at the part of the bed where he fell asleep, imagining to find him there at that moment.

I hurry to go to the bed and remove the pillow that I hugged when I missed him: I throw it in a corner of the cabinet, then open the drawer where I find my pajamas and take out all his shirts and sweatshirts, throwing them in the same corner of the closet.

I will not spend other nights imagining that I am sleeping by his side, I will not spend another second more of my life thinking about a man who does not deserve me. I put a hand on my belly, thinking about how unfortunate my twins are.

Alex will never be the father of my children, because he doesn't know how to love, but only to disappoint.

Chapter

29

I have been in front of the mirror for half an hour now, trying to follow Annarita's lessons and to wear makeup in a decent way, but I give up after a few attempts.
I want to show those around me that I am not a woman to play with, but one who can stand up to an asshole and domineering man.

The words he said to me on the evening of two weeks ago destroyed me, for a moment I even considered Catherine superior to me, but I try to convince myself that he doesn't deserve me

Through the mirror my eyes end up on the belly covered by a large sweatshirt, without being able to glimpse what is behind it.
I didn't tell him anything ...
And I begin to think it appropriate to tell him at another time, when he realizes the mistake he is making.
Also because we haven't talked to each other for fourteen days and since things have been getting worse for me: I didn't think my pregnancy would be so heavy, but in two weeks I threw up my soul. There will be no going back, not after that evening, when he decided to ruin the best day of my life.

At some point I even thought about letting go of his words and rushing to reproach him for being idiotic and irresponsible, I would have advised him to change his attitude and go back to reasoning clearly since he will become a father.
But then I went back to reality and remembered that Alex would never do such a thing, since he hasn't done it in six years.
He can only pretend, act to get what he wants, but when he returns to being himself he only knows how to hurt and get rid of what he really thinks.

I jump when my phone, abandoned on the bedside table, signals the arrival of a message. I sit on the bed, waiting to read a message from my mother, then I roll my eyes and think of how to convince her that it's not over between me and Alex.

I turn on the phone snorting, but I am amazed when I read Tiara's name on the screen: she may not know that I am pregnant and would like to tell her, but I also recently understood that with her I have to be careful with what I say, if I don't want it discover my mother too.
Alex must be the first to know and it doesn't rain on this, also because he could really go out of his mind if someone else found out.

* Sorry, Clara. Your mom overheard me talking to mine. "

I open my eyes: I was sure that my mother had called me because of Tiara, but I did not think Clelia knew that too.
I mentally curse Tiara, but then I realize that it's all my fault and my long tongue. I wanted to get rid of a weight that I did not get rid of regardless and, despite the proximity of John, Tiara, Annarita and, in his own way, Andrew, it seems to me that I cannot get out of this abyss.

The only thing that gives me a thread of joy in this medium is the emotion of becoming a mother of twins.

I thought I dreamed the moment I woke up in a hospital bed and received the good news, but John's message the next morning helped me realize that it was all true. And it is wonderful that, in all this mess that is burning my neurons, the green beans in the middle of my belly make me smile.

I go back to looking at the phone, while my eyes end up repeatedly on my father's name in the contacts: I haven't talked to him for a long time, since my mother doesn't give much space.

My father has always been a wise man and he taught me to solve every obstacle calmly: 'It is not a problem if you cannot solve it .'- he often said , and Alex's seems to be a really unsolvable mess, even if I put it all the calm that I have stored since childhood.
If he were here right now, he wouldn't even bother to talk to me, but he would go to Alex and make him think.

I shake my head and don't think much about it before I click on her number.

"Clara?" - she almost screams from the other side without letting the phone ring more than once. He seems surprised to hear me, most likely because I don't call him often. "Yes, dad, are you all right?" - my voice trembles when I hear hers.
How can I tell him that he will become a grandfather at a time when my things with Alex cannot be worse.
I would disappoint him greatly because I promised him to trust Alex, but I shouldn't have done it, on the contrary, I would have had to satisfy him and continue my life in the

Bronx, most likely working for one of the small neighborhood
hospitals.
"Sure. Are you okay? »- I think of the words of my mother,
who made me understand that Dad knows nothing about it.
«Y-Yes.» - the tone of my voice is more insecure than
necessary, but it does not insist.
I am not well, on the contrary, I would like to disappear from the
face of the earth, or at least go far. I want to get away from Alex to
make him understand what he has lost, who preferred sex with a
beautiful woman to the love I gave him.
I want to get away from him ... but I can't, and that's what
pisses me off.

I have my suitcase two meters away and I have everything I
need to start a new life.

Yet I don't do it because I'm a coward! I'm afraid to start all
over again alone in another city and with other friends.
I am an idiot because I hurt myself, preferring to watch him
touch Catherine rather than avoid everyone and hide
somewhere.

«Okay .» - he sighs, but I interrupt him:
«What would you do ... if suddenly I felt you ... suffocate?»
- my question is abstract and my father takes some time
before answering. «I would continue to do what I have
always done.
The problem is not you, Clara, but the people around
you. They are the ones who have to change their
attitude. " I nod to his words as if he could really see
me. "Already."
Needless to keep looking in the mirror to see what's wrong
with me, the problem is Alex and his pride.

«Do not make hasty decisions .» - he adds shortly after in a serious tone, almost foreseeing what I was going to do.
«Um, is Mum there with you?» - I quickly change the subject, hoping that my father will understand. «No!» - she answers quickly, while I look at the clock in confusion.
«Are you already at work?» - I ask puzzled. I wanted to clear up with her after yesterday's call. "Yes, he's working!" - the nervousness in my father's voice is obvious, since he can't lie, but I decide not to dwell on it.
"Can you tell her to ring me when she can call me?" - I add shortly after.
«I'll tell you, I 'll tell you.» - he says quickly and I can imagine him scratching the back of his neck uneasily. "All right. Dad we'll talk to you again. Thanks. »- I add serious, but does not answer, so I close the call shortly after.

I get up and look at my reflection again in the mirror, adjusting the disaster I made a little while ago, and then look at the clock that says eight in the evening.

I have to get out of this room, which is becoming more and more difficult every day, since I often meet Alex in the living room.
We do not speak to each other, except to quarrel, but neither of them intends to speak civilly to the other.
I open the door and then close it behind me, finding, as I imagined, Alex on the sofa while zapping from one channel to another.
If only I could, I would slap him every time I see him to get his attention and make him regret having lost me.
I reach the shelf if I cook to put an empty glass on it and fill it with apple juice.
«Are you going out?» - without my noticing Juliet takes a seat on the stool next to me, looking me straight in the eye.
I just nod, while I adjust the sweatshirt so as not to be noticed by the attentive gaze of the little girl. «Aren't you

going to work?» - eyes narrowed , making me almost choke on the liquid.

Neither of them, not even Alex, had noticed this detail: in two weeks nobody actually asked me why I wasn't going to the hospital, and obviously I didn't think about this detail.

I snap my head towards the man sitting in front of the television, hoping he hasn't overheard, but his eyes are on me.

"I took some days off." - I immediately think of the answer to the next question.

«You?» - raises an eyebrow, which does also his father, which does not look away.

I nod obviously, trying to show myself confident, but at the same time I beg Juliet not to insist, even if she doesn't want to know anything about it, since she continues to be an investigator:

"Who do you go out with?"

«With ... John.» - I shoot the first nonsense that comes to mind: I certainly cannot say in front of Alex that I am going to have dinner at Catherine's house, with her and her father. "I thought he was celebrating his anniversary with Andrew." - Alex's ironic tone makes my jaw clench as I cross his dark, indescribable eyes.

I don't answer, even if I try to formulate a sentence of complete meaning, but in all of them there is at least one dirty word, so I decide to shut up.

"Maybe you meant that you go out with Juliet's good teacher ." - he adds with disdain shortly after.

His attitude leads me to raise my chin up and look him in the eye as he has been watching me for a long time.

«Yes.» - I say serene, without moving an eyelash, while he holds the remote control between his fingers and shows the vein in his neck.

At one time I would have believed that this attitude was a sign that he loved me, but now I know it is only a sign of his pride. He realizes that I don't drool after him anymore, so he gets mad about being replaced.

"I don't think it's a problem." - I add to provoke him, but a word does not come from his lips.

He continues to stare intently at me, almost wanting to read me in thought and discover my intentions.

"Really?" - Juliet forces me to break that snare and turn my attention to her.

I nod, because in the end I'm going to have dinner at her father's house, so I'm not lying to her completely. I don't know, however, if Louis will be present, although I strongly hope that this is not the case, since we have not yet clarified.

He is responsible for that gesture and he has to take the first step, but I have never met him since that day, even when I was forced to give Juliet a ride to take her to school.

I turn my head upwards before entering my car, noting the starry sky without clouds: one evening, almost a month after the transfer, Alex returned home drunk and lay down in the middle of the garden looking towards the sky.

I should have been angry and told him four, but all I did was keep him company, while he was shooting nonsense without taking his eyes off the stars.

I lose myself so much at the memory of Alex's carefree expression that evening that I don't realize I am staring at a fixed point in the courtyard.

I shake my head and go back to reality, mentally slapping myself to be able to let go of flashbacks like that.

I turn on the car and start to retrace the same road that I
followed with my eyes clouded days ago, when I learned the
truth through Alex's mouth.
I was so enraged and disappointed that it was a miracle to get
to my destination alive. I never imagined I would make this
journey again to go and have dinner with her: everything will
go smoothly if Louis is not there and if I can pretend well in
front of the manager. I disappointed him enough with my
pregnancy, now I don't want to avoid satisfying him at least in
this way.

I can recognize the wooden gate from afar, which is easy
since it is the only brushstroke of blue in this neighborhood, so
I park the car a few meters away and mentally swear to have
bad luck.

It wasn't enough to have to feel bad for Alex's arrogance, but I also
found out that he cheated on me with a woman, who turns out to
be my boss's daughter and the sister of the man who kissed me
without Alex's knowledge. I ring the bell without waiting for my
conscience to repent and change my mind, and wait for the door
to open.
In the meantime I look around to make sure that Louis's car is
not there, but I don't have time to check carefully that the door
opens, showing a smiling and fake Catherine, not only for the
smile, but also for all that that has remade her body.
I look at her with an air of sufficiency, but then I notice her
father raise a hand behind her, then I transform my grimace
of disgust into a wide toothy smile.
«Come in, dinner is almost ready.» - he invites me ,
hiding the middle index that he gives me to his father.
I don't answer and I follow her heels:

«Good evening, boss.» - I salute him civilly, trying to contain
my instinct to slap the beautiful (and redone) face of your
daughter.
I notice the latter wearing a black lace dress with a deep
neckline near the breast and not overly short.
He seems to want to boast of his shapes and his long model
legs.
I lower my head looking at myself and noting that I can't even
compare myself to Catherine: I wear a pair of slightly wider
jeans than usual so as not to cling to my stomach and a
sweatshirt that reaches my mid-thigh, which I can enter three
times.
I cross my arms over my chest as a sign of pride, and then
follow the two of them through the corridor of this gigantic
house.

Strange that Catherine does not have a separate home,
given the wealth of her father, and this also applies to Louis,
who also has a good job.

I look around as if I have never seen a more beautiful house in
my life, until we arrive in a room with a table set in the center.
«Please, dear.» - I would like to throw up for the fake
kindness of Catherine who, after glancing at her father,
almost checking that he is looking at her, moves a chair
away from the table, indicating me to sit down.
I fear that if I open my mouth, nothing pleasant will come out,
so I just reach out and take a seat on the chair.

«Guadalupe!?» - I start when he starts screaming with his aggressive
goose voice the name of a woman, who shortly after appears behind
me.
«Yes, Mrs. Catherine ...» - she begins to say, but, without
letting her finish, the blonde says in an authoritarian tone:
«You can start serving dinner.» - she says, without looking
into her eyes, then the poor woman leaves head down.

I can imagine what torture that woman is subjected to by working for a witch like Catherine. I bet if Catherine had a husband ...
I shake my head, realizing that I'm exaggerating.

"So, Catherine, do you have anything to say to Clara?" - the old man sitting on the short side of the table urges his daughter to speak, while I prepare to attend a theater scene:
"Yes sure. Clara, I really apologize for how I behaved that day. I was not in myself and ... »- he begins to say crossing his hands as if he is praying. I interrupt her before I spit them in the eye:
"We're ... okay. There is no need to complicate the situation. »- my cheeks start to hurt as much as he is smiling forcefully.

He does not answer and fortunately not even his father intrudes, while a room places the first courses in front of us. The first thing I notice is that the dishes are gigantic, but the portions are not that great, so much so that I could eat the salad and the dish, but still not be full.
Tonight me and the twins will suffer, but we should endure until we return home, where I will manage many other crap.

I take the fork first with the intention of starting to eat that food for aristocrats, but as soon as I do to bring the salad to my mouth, Catherine screams, opening her eyes wide, which immediately makes me drop the fork of a frightened hand.
«No!» - he adds, while I put a hand on my chest. "What's wrong?" - his father intervenes for me.

"Don't start eating! There is still one person missing . »- only now do I notice the extra plate by his side and I immediately think it is Louis.
Cabbages! I thought I was saved, but this dinner will prove more embarrassing than it already is.

I lower my head, blushing when the bell rings and one of the staff women walks towards the corridor leading to the front door.
"There he is! He has arrived. »- Catherine stands up to meet him, while I mentally curse myself for not having found an excuse and not coming.
When the sound of Catherine's heels becomes louder and annoying, a sign of the fact that she has returned with the new and unwanted guest, I decide to raise my head so as not to be rude.
But I would have preferred not to have done so when my eyes meet Alex's gaze, standing in front of me and with an arm around Catherine's hips ...

Chapter 30

He looks at me with a confused and surprised expression at the same time, while his arm remains around Catherine's pelvis.

I immediately take my eyes off the two at the exact moment
when she approaches her cheek with her lips.

He didn't expect to see me here tonight, he thought I was
really going out with Louis, and he remains like an idiot staring
at Catherine's bare skin with his hand.

Without thinking twice, I take the half-filled glass of wine and bring it
to my lips, regardless of the fact that I am pregnant.
If I knew I could find him here I would have been even more
convinced to come: I really want to see them flirting before my
eyes and reproach myself who Alex really is.
«I didn't know there would be a guest.» - Catherine's
father gets up and goes to my chair, taking the glass
of wine out of my hand and glancing at me.
I roll my eyes secretly, while the two take their places in front
of me.
Other than wine, now I would need something strong that I
have never tried before and that can help me pretend for
nothing for the rest of the evening.
I look sideways at Alex upset, while the woman at his side
takes him by the arm:

"Yup. Dad, let me introduce you to my boyfriend. »-
Catherine's words hit me straight in the face.

I snap my head upwards with my eyes wide open, crossing
Alex's.
Her expression is indecipherable, although I try to dig into her
eyes to understand if Catherine is telling the truth.

He doesn't answer. Do not deny his words. It does not
contradict it.

I put a hand on my belly without realizing it immediately, while I already feel my eyes pinching: I do not take my eyes away and he imitates me, avoiding Catherine who tries to attract her attention.

It took him a year to tell me I was his, but it took him a week to replace me with another woman.

I let myself be touched by you, I allowed you to kiss and sleep by my side, considering you the man of my life!
I felt protected by your arms, when in reality I
had to protect myself from you! I wanted a
family from you! I'm pregnant with you ...

I will not allow my children to have a father like that, one who changes his mind at any moment and who is unable to carry on a relationship.
I suffered a lot for him, I even risked losing my parents, but in vain.
He has become attached to another woman, I have already tired him, regardless of how much I can cry on myself and regret having let myself go in front of him.
I continue to look at him even though his eyes are turned away, while he smiles showing the dimples that have always left me breathless.
He wears a dark shirt with the first free buttons, showing the tattoos I've kissed every night since the first time we made love.
I regret having left a mark on his skin, even if it will be one of many for him.

I would also like to erase every second spent with his body on mine, every sensation that his bare skin has traced on mine, every memory of his body united with mine, every moan, but I can't ... because now every millimeter of my skin reports his name.

I lower my head to my belly, but the more I think of the twins
the more I feel like suffocating myself in this room, while I
breathe its own air.

"I apologize. The bathroom? »- I ask in a low voice.
«Are you all right?» - the old man forces me to look up, while I
adjust the sweatshirt.
I simply nod, trying to form a smile with my lips, but what
comes out is a forced grimace.

I need some air.

«I'll take you .» - Catherine starts to get up, but Alex takes her
by the arm and forces her to sit next to her again.

"Accompany her!" - the chief calls a waitress who puts her
hand on my back, indicating to follow her.

I hold back the storm that is raging in me until I reach the
bathroom: before I even get in I get rid of the tears that
wanted to come out from the moment Alex arrived.
I lean on the sink, regardless of the cleaning lady behind me,
and look at myself in the mirror for an indefinite time.
I watch the salty drops fall down my cheeks and wonder what I
have done to be treated this way.
I don't deserve it.

They look perfect together, she is an elegant, harlot but
elegant woman, while Alex remains a Greek god who attracts
the attention of every woman around him.
I, on the other hand, am dressed as a picnic in the mountains
and cannot draw two lines of black pencil around the eyes.

They are both assholes and bullies, they think only of themselves and
believe themselves superior to those around them.

But I'm not inferior: my father said that it's not my
fault, but whoever is around me. It is not me that is
not enough, but it is not enough for Alex, so he goes
in search of adventurous women.

I introduce you to my boyfriend ... Catherine's words repeat
themselves in my mind, causing me a severe headache.
A burning in the throat forces me to hurry and bend over to the
bidet, waiting to empty my stomach before I even eat.

I get rid of the vomit and the tears as quickly as possible, and
then rinse my face and pretend a smile in front of the mirror.

I keep my lips bent up until I show up again in the room,
finding everyone intent on eating.
"Clara ..." - I stop myself when I notice the presence of Louis
sitting on the chair next to me. At this moment I would like to
raise my eyes to heaven: this dinner could not really be
worse!

The smile dies on my lips when he gets up at the same time
that Alex drops a fork on the ground and clenches his fists.
"Lou- Louis ..." - I whisper more to myself than to him.
If he only hinted the kiss in front of those present it would
trigger an uproar.
I go towards him, leaving out Alex's attitude, while
the father smiles relaxed. As soon as I approach
her body I kiss a kiss on her cheek as a sign of
greeting, and then go to her ear and whisper:
«Pretend nothing, please!» - I beg him , mentally thanking the
primary for attracting the attention of the other two.
But out of the corner of my eye I observe that Alex, unlike
Catherine, has his gaze turned towards Louis, almost wanting
to incinerate him with his eyes, but he does not move an inch.

And he would do well to continue to contain himself, since now
... he's engaged.

«Okay .» - he just says, lowering his eyes at the same time he returns sitting.

I imitate him slowly, clearing my throat and glancing quickly at the man sitting in front of me. If before his expression was indecipherable, now he is definitely angry, as indicated by the fact that he drinks the liquid inside in one breath of the glass between his fingers.

I raise an eyebrow, almost threatening him to stop doing my own business and to fill his woman with attentions, instead of continuing to stare at me.

«You can also serve yourself. »- I return to reality when I notice that the primary invites us to eat. I quickly take my fork and lower my head onto my plate.

"When did you meet ?" - he continues to ask his daughter, completely unconscious of the fact that Alex was the reason for our dispute.

I almost choke on the salad, thinking about how to avoid every single word that will come out of Catherine's mouth, because I know it will hurt me, even if I admit that I want to listen to every detail of their story by thread and by sign.

I want to know how long I've been stabbed in the back.

«We met at work, when I told you that there was a newcomer ...» - her shrill voice fills the room, while I listen carefully, bringing my eyes to Alex, who seems to be too busy recording something on the phone, but then Catherine draws her attention by bringing her fingers to the back of her neck.

I tighten my jaw and bite the inside of my cheek so as not to scream in my face not to touch it.

Alex nods to her words and lets her play with her hair while I say inside.

«Since that day we have always worked together and, after a few little arrows ...» - I clench my fingers around the fork, imagining to poke an eye at that exact moment, but I force myself not to look up to follow the movements of his fingers.

"... we started going out."

«Since when?» - I intervene interrupting her, realizing too late that I have spoken.

Everyone's eyes end up on my figure and I do everything to not look at Alex's side, but against my will I watch him sideways, turn my attention away from the phone to turn it to me, suddenly interested in the conversation undertaken by Catherine .

Cross your arms over your chest, highlighting your neck muscles, and tilt your head. «Just out of curiosity.» - I add shortly after, making myself small in the chair and hiding in my sweatshirt. I have to learn to curb my emotions, although it would be difficult now that I have hormones that work madly for pregnancy.

I go back to eating in silence, while the waitresses bring the first courses, pretending to be uninterested in Catherine's answer.

I can imagine the satisfied expression in the latter, since among his intentions there was obviously that of annoying me and making me understand that Alex is his property now.

" Almost six months ." - every single muscle in my body freezes, making me unable to make any movement.
I raise my head slowly, but not to look at Catherine.
Corrugo faced him and opened his mouth wide as my eyes met Alex's.

«Er, okay. I hope things will go well between you and that there are no obstacles, I address you above all, son. »- the words of the primary are the last I hear, while I think about what his daughter said.

Six months!!
I was betrayed for six months straight without even realizing it
...
I look at Alex as if I were in front of a monster: who knows how many times I told him to love him after they were seen up with Catherine.

"Well, it's difficult, boss. I tell you from personal experience .
»- I answer the primary instead of Catherine, while the smile falls from the lips of the latter.

«It won't happen, I assure you. If I want something, I get it. »- Catherine's answer seems to be a threat, while Alex glares at me, almost supporting her.
"That's what I said too." - I whisper, turning more to myself and Alex, rather than to her.

"Do you have a man, Clara?" - the primary changes the subject, displacing me with a simple question. I had a man. The one who replaced me with your daughter and who now has the courage to look serious in the eyes, while before she seemed to want to electrocute me.

I shake my head, fearing to open my mouth to say something to regret, but then I decide to speak to break the awkward silence that has arisen.

«No.» - there is a word that makes it clear to those who are in front of me this moment. Her chest swings up and down quickly, while she keeps her gaze fixed on my puddles. "I believe it. With the sweatshirt, honey, you do not even marry the bum more desperate to ... "- the Catherine's voice is interrupted by that of his brother, I had even

forgotten that it was by my side: " Cat! "- opens the eyes
reproachfully, while she shrugs and her father sighs, giving
her a dirty look.
«For now, no, who knows in the future ... Maybe I will find someone who will
be so in love with me as to marry me
and remain faithful throughout my life. »- I spit sour, without
looking at the recipient of my words, even though I know he is
looking at me right now.
I can hear his sighs, a sign of frustration and I imagine the
anger in his eyes, which will now be so dark as to be scary.

Nobody answers my words immediately, so I start to focus on
the fish dish that invites me to devour it.

«I would marry you .» - I jerk my head, and with me the others
present, towards Louis who looks at me with a serious
expression.
"How-what?" - I manage to whisper, while
her lips form a tender smile. I try to imitate
it, but the corners of my mouth remain
downward.
«And who wouldn't want to? You are beautiful,
kind and a surgeon. »- he adds, follow his
father:« He is right. »- he admits shrugging his
shoulders and supporting his son's words.
I would have burst out laughing at Louis' words right now, if it
hadn't been for the kiss he gave me unexpectedly and that
makes this moment very embarrassing.
I continue to stare at it, and then return to reality when I feel
my elbow getting wet and a stink of wine invade my nostrils,
after a sudden thump:
«Sorry, it was an accident.» - I jerk my head towards Alex who
pretends to be sorry for the mess he made on the table,
causing the bottle of wine to fall open.
I glare at him as he shrugs his shoulders with mock
innocence, at the exact moment when two waitresses
approach, then turns his attention to Louis.

He starts to get up and help me dry the sweatshirt, but I block
it with one hand:
«Don't worry , it's nothing.» - I snort mentally, while the
headmaster shifts his attentive gaze from me to Alex.
«Come on, I'll get you my shirt.» - sent me to follow him
to his room, but this time it's Alex who interrupts him:
"She only got her arm wet, I didn't take a shower."
«You can be more careful.» - Louis turns his eyes on the
figure of Alex, almost challenging him, while I open my eyes: it
is not convenient for him to be the hero in front of him,
because if there is one thing that Alex can do well it is being
impulsive and aggressive.

I see him in his eyes that he does everything to avoid getting
up from his chair and hurling himself at Louis, but in the end
his pride wins: he gets up from the chair in the blink of an eye,
followed by Catherine who tries to stop him, but he doesn't He
succeeds.
He goes around the table in two steps to find himself in
front of Louis, so I don't think twice before I stand
between the two and defend the man behind me.

In doing so I find myself in front of two bloodshot eyes that
look at me furiously and threatening to move away from there.
I hear the doctor's chair crawl, a sign that he stands up too:
"Boy, calm down and go back to your seat." - he says in a very
relaxed tone of voice, but that has no effect on the man two
centimeters from my face.
I don't move an inch, forgetting why I'm standing in front of
Louis, and I get lost in front of that image. He hates me...
He despises me as if he had never had anything to do with me
and as if I had not been by his side for years.

She looks at me like a stranger, making me feel guilty even though I'm the real victim in this medium "Don't you dare touch her!" - Louis steps forward, but I hurry to raise an arm.
They're really trying to protect me from Alex ...
Only now do I realize that it has become a danger to be kept away.
I try to return the expression, but I don't have the time: as soon as Louis finishes talking, Alex tightens his jaw and starts to reach him, taking my elbow and pushing me to his right.
"I kill you!"
I shiver at the tone of her voice, without immediately realizing that I have a piece of furniture in front of her, until I hit one of her corners and lose my balance.
I find myself suddenly with my face on the ground and severe pain under my belly, while the primary runs to my rescue.
I feel everyone's eyes on me, but mine desperately look for Alex's.
He leaves the collar of Louis' shirt, initially petrified with two puddles that still express anger towards me.
As soon as he meets my frightened gaze, he assumes a worried expression and runs in my direction, while the chair beside him falls due to his sudden movement: he kneels on the ground dilating the pupils.
Without realizing his quick moves, he takes my face in his powerful hands. «Baby ...» - she begins to say, but a second cramp makes me take a grimace of pain, reminding me of the twins.

'My babies!'

C
h
a
p
t
e
r

3
1

My babies! '- I think immediately, while my hand ends up on
my stomach.

«Did you hurt yourself?» - Alex's eyes reach my hand, where
he brings his squeezing my fingers between his.
They raise their arm immediately, leaving his hand on my
belly.
No as soon as I notice that gesture, a trail of shivers traces
my spine: he looks at me worried, tracing an imaginary line
with his thumb on my sweatshirt.

Her pupils are so clear right now, while her face is a few
inches from mine, but Catherine approaches and rests her
hand on her shoulder.
"Is fine. Come. »- tries to bring him back to reality, but his eyes
do not leave mine, as if there was no one else around us.

"I'll take you to the emergency room." - avoids Catherine and
starts to bring one arm behind my back and the other under
my legs.
"No! Take off your hands! I'm fine. »- I scream, standing up.

For a moment I forgot who I was facing: I can't go to the hospital with him. He cannot know that I am pregnant, let alone now that he is engaged to Catherine.
I'd be selfish if I avoided telling him the truth, and I'll tell him, but not now ...
If I told him, it would seem like a way to get him back to me, but I don't want to deal with him anymore, regardless of the feeling that still binds me to him.
I leave him kneeling on the ground and reach my place: he is just a proud man who cannot restrain himself. He's only good at making trouble!
«Clara, it would be better to check ... being inci ...» -
I open my eyes to the voice of the primary, interrupting him before he can say what I don't want Alex to know.
«I will come tomorrow morning. I just fell. »- he gives me a knowing look, but he is still upset. The moments of silence that follow are always broken by the voice of the blonde behind me, who still tries to convince Alex to get up and return to their place:
«Louis, you had better keep your mouth shut.» - I can imagine how furious she is right now, while I even feel guilty.
He let Alex into his bed knowing that he was engaged to myself. Louis does not respond to his threat, but resumes sitting down and looking sideways at me.

I feel so out of place right now that I would like to disappear from this house as soon as possible, without having to face the reason for my problems again.
I would prefer him to sit there, behind my chair all evening so as not to risk meeting his eyes again, but I feel him get up and, pushed by the woman at his side, start again on the opposite side of the table.

I go back to eating in silence, but nobody around the table can pretend that nothing has happened: "I understand everything."

- the primary resumes talking after moments of awkward
silence, while he nods to his words, but then adds nothing.
He understood everything.
He understood that his daughter is a viper who has decided to
present him with his new conquest tonight, to reproach me
that Alex has chosen her.
And maybe he also realized that either twins carry the asshole's
chromosomes sitting in front of me. I close in on myself for the rest
of the dinner, thinking of Alex's gesture that touched me at the point
where his children grow up at this moment and I imagine the same
gesture at another time, in another place.

If all this hadn't happened, Alex and I would most likely be
on the couch watching television and eating junk food.
But then he turns his gaze from the screen to me, who eats
fried chicken wings and bought at the take & go two meters
from our house, most likely I did not want to cook.
I am dirty with oil and Worchestershire sauce everywhere on
my face, but he continues to stare at me as if I were more
beautiful than the protagonist of the film we watch.
'What 's up?' - I ask with my mouth full, but he doesn't answer.
Stretch your arm towards my swollen belly, raising one corner
of your mouth.
'They are kicking my hand .'- he laughs and then suddenly
approaches and leaves a quick kiss on my nose.
He does not go away, on the contrary, he continues to sigh on
my lips, and then press his mouth against mine. I feel the
softness of her lips sucking on my skin, while the tip of her
tongue moistens the corner of my mouth ....

"It's late! I have to go. »- I get up quickly, interrupting the
conversation between father and son, but above all erasing
my perverse thoughts.
With all my strength, I avoid Alex's gaze and limit myself to
turning my heels, despite the primary rising to his feet with the
intention of convincing me to wait.

My eyes start to burn again and I feel the tears coming, while I arrive at a padded step in front of the door so as not to show myself in such with them in front of them.
I hurry to open the front door, but I jump when I hear quick steps behind me :
"Wait for me!" - recognizing Louis' voice I stop at the door threshold, with my hand on the handle. I don't turn to his side, although I don't blame him for what happened a little while ago. «I'll take you to the car.» - I don't answer and I let him open the door for me.

Finally I feel I can breathe freely and fill my lungs with air, while I close my eyes and feel the wind hit my face.
If before I liked the smell of the earth wet from the rain, now it makes my nose turn up in annoyance. «I didn't want to provoke that reaction in him, I 'm sorry.» - it is clear from the tone of his voice that he was undecided whether or not to open this speech, but it would have been ridiculous not to talk about it.
I feel my throat dry and I seem unable to speak: on the one hand I would have preferred to be alone and get lost in thoughts, but I am also afraid of spending time in solitude. If I go on like this I will be locked up in an asylum sooner or later. "Er ..." - I cleared my throat and then thought about what to say.
"I shouldn't have come." - I admit sincerely.
I shouldn't have been here because I knew that Catherine was going to plot something, all the more so because she pretended to be kind and welcoming even before Alex arrived. I shouldn't have introduced myself because, however little I know him, I knew he would come and do what he's doing.
«Instead you did well. We both know I didn't want to ... kiss you that day that way. I'm so sorry, I would not want us to be uncomfortable. »- he starts to say, but seems to contradict himself, since he brings his hand to the back of his neck and lowers his eyes on the ground, avoiding my gaze.

It is obvious that we could not go back to being friends as before, but I like to spend my time with him, regardless of his gesture.
So far he has always inspired me with confidence, he has even helped me with Giulietta, making me understand his strange behavior.

«I'm pregnant.» - I suddenly spit , as if she asked me or I felt obliged to tell her. I do it because I want to tell someone after so long, I want to feel like a spoiled pregnant woman and maybe I

want to share these emotions with someone other than John, who is extremely happy and does not understand my concerns, but continues to buy gifts for twins who are not yet born and whose sex I do not know.

"Oh, Wow!" -
stops on the
spot, widening
his eyes.
«Yes.» - I sigh,
waiting for his
amazement.
"Of..."

«Alex.» - I conclude in his place,
while he assumes a pensive
expression. I shouldn't have told
him: who knows what he's thinking
of me now.

«And he doesn't know.» - analyzes as if he
were saying it to himself and I was not next
to him. I don't answer and bite the inside of

my cheek so as not to let the tears come
out:

"Two big problems will await you ." - he says, while I close my
eyes.
I don't want to hear about problems, but I give him time to
continue before replying:
«One: you have to decide his name as soon as possible!» - I
snort and start to reply, but then I frown, realizing what he just
said.
My expression turns into an amused grimace and, for the first
time that evening, indeed, for so many days, I laugh
spontaneously.
I was expecting something like: 'you will have to grow up the
trouble alone' or 'it will be difficult to get the job back', but for
him the real problem will be to decide how to call them. "Do
not laugh! My grandparents divorced because of me. One
wanted to call me Hardin and the other Jack. "- he continues
to have a serious face, which amuses me even more.
"But your name is Louis."
«In fact, in the end my mother decided .» - he says
nostalgically, while I can't stop smiling. "The second
problem?" - I ask curious.
"The diapers!" - I start laughing at the exact moment I get in
the car and start the engine.
«Do you know how much you have to spend with diapers in a
month for a newborn?!» - he asks ironically, while he also
keeps from laughing.
«There are two.» - I say proud, jokingly raising my head.
«Capers!» - he takes a step back, but then he returns serious,
leaning in front of the window. «It's great news, believe me.» -
he winks at me, reassuring me a lot, and then he returns to his
former position.
I raise a hand to greet him and happy with his unusual
reaction, keeping my smile, without even realizing it, for a
piece of the road.

But then the mind takes me back to what happened before I
left his home.

It was the most unpleasant evening of my life: I was humiliated
by Catherine for the second time in front of her father and I
allowed Alex to get too close.
So much so that now I can't think of anything but his
damned eyes that looked at me as if he really cared about
me.
I leave everything out, even the fact that it risked hurting me
and his children, and I relive the moment when he catapulted
me onto my body.
It has always been like this: Alex has made a lot of trouble, he
has always put me in difficult conditions to overcome, but then
he didn't run away.
He came back in one way or another to help me get out of
the tunnel: he did damage, but then he tried to fix it himself.

I don't know why I still think he really feels something for me:
he got engaged to Catherine, but continues to look at me as if
I belonged to him, as if he didn't want to sit next to her in that
dinner.

But I'm just torturing myself.
Is this how it feels not to be reciprocated?
It can't be the same: I tried what it means to kiss him and
have it on my body, I tried the effect that makes his lips feel
on my skin, I know every detail of his body, every mole, every
tattoo.

I realize that I have arrived at my destination only when I pass
my house, then I snort loudly and go looking for a roundabout
or a road to go back.

I start to scold myself: I have to stop thinking about someone
who doesn't deserve to be important to me.
He doesn't deserve me, I understood this well, but I must learn
to stand up to him and not to distract myself, as has often
happened lately.

Forget it! As soon as I arrive at these conclusions I find
myself in front of Alex's car, parked in front of the gate.
We were missing an inch and I would have run into it.

Fortunately I stop the car in time without hurting myself during
braking, but I also notice a more serious danger: Alex is inside
that house and I don't want to face it.
The first thing that comes to my mind right now is not to go in
and spend the night in the car, or to go to John, being sure that it
would not be a nuisance for him, but then I shake my head and I
realize that I have returned there. same coward as before, who
runs away, instead of facing moment like this with her head held
high.

I quickly get out of the car, after having collected the keys, and
tighten my jaw, forcing me to think about the worst moments
of the dinner.
Among these I repeat the moment when Catherine announced
their engagement and the blood starts to boil in my veins.

I open the door without thinking twice and it surprises me not
to find it in front of the television with the remote control in
one hand and a beer in the other.
I frown, but I don't care, as I head for the kitchen.
I almost scream in fright when I find Alex in front of the fridge,
intent on taking a bottle of water, but he stops when he
realizes my presence.

I do not give him time to meet my gaze which takes my eyes
off his figure and aspect which moves from the fridge.
Without saying anything he moves away from the latter and
leans on the kitchen counter, but without stopping to stare
at me as he opens the bottle and starts drinking.
I take his place and out of the corner of my eye, I see him glue
his lips to the bottle, then I shake my head and bring my
attention inside the refrigerator.
The first thing I notice is that there are too many
vegetables: why did I go crazy for this crap? I have to do
the shopping and I need meats, cheeses, but also chips,
marchmellow and cherries. Thinking about cherries I get a
craving for strawberry jam tart, I don't know why.

But for the moment I have to settle for a slice of pizza
abandoned by Juliet, fortunately.

I still feel his presence behind me and I wonder why he hasn't
already gone away: it even annoys me to look him in the face
after what has happened, so much so that I can't keep my
mouth shut ;:

"Strange that you came back so early. I thought you were going to spend the
night with Catherine. "

He doesn't answer while I decide not to turn to his side, but
I can imagine his upset or furious expression.
If before he only felt his deep breathing, now it seems he has
even stopped breathing.

"Would anything change for you ?" - his question comes out in
a whisper.
«Of course not.» - I find the courage to turn to his side and
look him straight in the eye, noting his puzzled face: he seems

surprised by my answer, almost regretful of the question he asked me.

"Ah, I forgot to wish you well! You and Catherine are made for each other. »- I take a bite of the pizza waiting for a reaction that doesn't come.

He shakes hands in two fists, but his expression still remains thoughtful.

"I hope your new relationship will last longer than the previous one." - I conclude bitterly and decide to finish eating in my room.

I give him a last grim look, then start to move towards the living room, but before leaving the kitchen he grabs my wrist, forcing me to turn back to him and look at him: in his eyes I read a great desperation, almost wanted to beg me not to leave:

«Clara, don't ...» - he begins to whisper, but I move immediately, freeing myself from his light grip, and I don't let him finish, with the fear that anything he would have said would have destroyed me.

C
h
a
p
t
e
r

3
3

I quickly leave the bed and start running towards the bathroom with the vomit minted. Fortunately, I manage to reach the toilet before I send out everything I ate yesterday and this morning at three.

I take a deep breath to fill my lungs with air, then get up and drain the water.

I return exhausted and annoyed to the kitchen, where I find Juliet standing and looking me straight in the eye. I hope he didn't hear my moans while I was throwing up, but it wouldn't be said by his shocked face. «Hey!» - I greet you with a wave of my hand and with a fake smile.
"Are you okay?" - his question leaves me puzzled and I immediately think of a justification. "I woke up with a stomach ache." - I explain, and then immediately feel guilty. I don't want to lie to you, but I can't even tell you that you will have brothers. He looks at me intensely making me uncomfortable:
"I believe it. With all the crap you've been eating lately ... You've also got a little tummy. »- she looks down, while I mentally slap myself for forgetting to wear something wider.
I hurry to turn my back and go in search of cereals.
I shrug my words, without finding the courage to look her in the eyes: if she wasn't just a tenyear-old girl she would surely have noticed that this is not a bloated belly for the food I eat.

I mentally beg you not to insist on this, so I try to change the subject:
"How's it going with your boyfriend?" - I pour milk into a bowl, continuing to spy on it out of the corner of my eye.
For the first time in a long time I see her use the phone often:

"We had a fight last night." - I roll my eyes: I begin to believe that men have the instinct to make women angry in DNA.
"Is it serious?" - I ask, but shrugs:
«I don't know if to forgive him.» - I grimace when I realize I put too many cereals in the milk. "I'm sorry."

"I told him I died for him ." - I suddenly turn to his side.
I look her straight in the eye to see if it really is a coincidence
or if she heard me speak to Alex last night.
"Do you think I have to forgive him?" - his expression is
indecipherable, while I don't find an answer to be able to
satisfy her.
I remain silent while I lower my eyes to the ground:
«Clara, promise me that you and my brother will make
peace.» - he continues leaving me speechless once again.
I put a hand in my hair and start talking, but I still don't know
what to say, so I end up snorting.
"I swear I didn't tell him anything about the
kiss between you and Louis, I don't ..." - I
shake my head at his words, reassuring
her.
«No, you have nothing to do with it.» - I just say with
a whisper, while I lean on the sink. "Um, don't you
have to go to school?" - I clear my throat.
She nods absentmindedly and I thank her mentally for not
continuing to ask me questions that I

can't answer, or that I don't want to answer in order not to
disappoint her, but she remains perplexed as I let her wait for me to
change her pajamas.

I bite my lower lip, realizing that Alex is not at home, but I
avoid wondering where he can be at this moment and where
he spent the night.
I look at the messy sofa and stop before I realize it to look at it.
It's been so long since I sit on it, since Catherine was
presented for the first time in this house, but now I can not
help but get closer and bend open sheets.
I grab them with my trembling hand, since my nostrils
immediately fill with her perfume. "It's horrible!" - I exclaim,
while Alex smiles secretly.
"Then we 'll take it." - I roll my eyes while he laughs with the
elderly saleswoman.

"It's grey! It's so sad ... »- I continue to look at him, perplexed,
trying in the meantime to convince me that it's not so bad.
"It's just a sofa." - Alex continues to show dimples and
his fun begins to annoy me. "Wait, I'll send a photo to
Tiara and Jessica." - I say it more to myself than to
him.

"If you stop hugging my brother's sheets, maybe I'll really get
to school in time ." - tries to hide a smile, as it makes me come
back to reality.
I shake my head and blush in his presence in front of me.
"Huh? Yes, I'm coming! »- I turn my heels and across the
hall, even risking to hit the edge of the table.

Return to her after five minutes:
«Sweatshirts are back to your liking.» - she looks at me with
amusement from head to toe, and only now do I realize how
much she resembles her father, not only for her physical
appearance.
«You don't know how much.» - I whisper, while I hug myself in
the jacket as soon as the wind becomes fiercer outside the
house.
I put my hand on her shoulder, then hold her bag with the
other, urging her to reach the badly parked car.

I have memorized this road for how often I have traveled it and
I would miss all this if I had to return to America or move
home.

I start to think of the solutions as the transfer, since even just
breathing the same air of Alex disturbs me.
But the idea of leaving that house forever hurts me even more: I
remember how excited I was to have a house all to myself and

from the first meeting with the real estate agent I realized how much I loved that building.

It was the perfect house for me, indeed for us, it was small but beautiful, secluded but welcoming and I customized every square meter. If I leave, I know what will happen: Catherine would come to live with Alex and change everything, starting with the pink painted walls, and I will not allow that to happen.

When my parents know that I am pregnant without getting married, or at least without being with Alex, they will threaten me to return to them.

And this option is what scares me most, because I love everything in Sydney, from the Darling Harbor aquarium to the Taronga zoo, from Hyde Park to the Olympic Park, from the bar near my house to the Sydney Cove Oyster Bar.

«Thanks for the ride.» - I park the car near the usual tree, while Juliet opens the door: "Ah! Things between me and my boyfriend are going great, anyway! »- she shows her tongue laughing, and then runs away, while I roll my eyes. The cunning of that girl sometimes scares me.

I start to move, shaking my head, but a voice interrupts me: "Clara! Stop for a moment! »- it doesn't take me long to understand that the voice belongs to Louis, so I look around to look for him with my eyes.

I can see it among the mass of pupils running towards my car, with a smile on their lips. "Do you have plans today?" - he asks, lowering himself to the window.

I don't even think about it and shake my head, thinking that I have left a check-up appointment with the gynecologist in the afternoon.

«In the morning I am free.» - I nod to my words, while he opens the door and takes a seat next to me, making me take on a frowning expression.

'I'll take you to a place. I'm sure you will like it. »- she winks at me, while I smile at her kindness. «Better than spending the morning watching Two and a half man and eating cheese chips .» - I shrug my shoulders with conviction.

"Where are you taking me ?" - I add, as I start driving towards a destination unknown to me. "It will be a surprise. I asked Juliet and she told me that you usually spend your free time there. »- I frown : I spend my free time at home cleaning or healing FoxLife.

Before this mess every time Alex was at home, so often, I had fun provoking him to make him remove that monotonous expression from his face, but apparently someone else thought about making him have fun, besides me.

"I just hope there are strawberry pies in this place ." - I think aloud, while he seems to think about it:

"I don't think so, but if you want later we can go to a restaurant."

"Then I understand!" - I exclaim, while he opens his eyes wide, with a look like 'how did you do ?!'. "What did you understand?" - he asks, narrowing his eyes.

«We are not going to a restaurant.» - I jokingly say , while he rolls his eyes.

«Insightful.» - he laughs, then adds - «You have to turn right.»
I follow his instructions, until I find myself in large buildings, never seen before.

I thought I knew every corner of Sydney, but I've never been to this place. I don't understand what is particular about this place, if not the arrival of the monorail.

"Follow me, Juliet said that you like museums, but that you have never visited it." - indicates a building that reads Powerhouse Museum.

I quickly think of a way to punish Juliet as soon as I meet her at home:
she knows that I hate museums and that I have never set foot in any
of the famous ones in Sydney: it is obvious that he shamelessly lied to
Louis and that he did it on purpose to make him look bad. From Louis'
bright eyes it is impossible not to pretend to be surprised and happy:
«I've never been there, it's true.» - I mentally curse that girl, while I
follow him inside that gigantic structure.
I try to encourage myself, thinking that maybe it won't go so bad, especially
in the company of Louis.

«This is the main room .» - he says completely taken, while I
absently look around, finding everything: astronaut costumes,
locomotives, computers ...
"This is one of the oldest engines invented by Watt and still
running." - I try to listen to his words and be careful of the story,
but I get distracted at the first sentence and look forward to
finishing the history lesson.

I look sideways at the ten o'clock clock and remember leaving
the house in a crazy mess, I even forgot the milk out of the
fridge.
I have to think about how to spend time now that I can't
work: one thing to do will surely be to review the notes of
the specialization meetings.
I can spend the rest of the day cooking ... and then I can eat
what I cooked. The important thing is not to stay with your
hands and get lost in thoughts: I no longer have to think about
Alex and his rebuilt doll.

«Let's go over there.» - he raises his chin indicating a
structure that I later learn to call
EcoHouse. I nod as I already feel my stomach rumbling loudly.
I can't wait to go to that
restaurant and devour the strawberry cake that Louis
promised me: I will be offended if it is not on the menu, which
is very difficult in Sydney.

The twins are really taking me to eat everything, but if I used to like vegetables before, now I
can't see them, even if they are the only thing I can't digest.
I go back to thinking seriously about what Louis said to me last night: I have to seriously think of a name to give to the little ones.

"Do you believe it?" - Louis's voice forces me to reopen my eyes suddenly.
"Uh? Yes, wow! »- I nod exaggeratedly, while my stomach begs to be filled.
«I'll show you one last thing!» - grabs my hand in an unexpected gesture that makes me shiver and drag me to another corner.
I watch Louis' fingers crossed over mine.
"Take my hand!" - I look at him badly, as he watches a tall young woman pass by. «Don't be jealous.» - Alex laughs, as if she did it on purpose, but I don't trust her.
I take his hand furiously and make the palms of our hands coincide and intersect our fingers. I laugh secretly noticing how small my hand is compared to his.

"I hope you enjoyed the exhibit." - I divert my thoughts to bring my attention to Louis, who looks at me intently.
They move their hand away from his to bring a lock of hair behind his ear:

«I will definitely return. Next time with Giulietta . »- I try to be as convincing as possible and seems to be satisfied with my reaction.
«Come on, the cake is waiting for us .» - he hurries towards the exit with me behind him, but this time I really follow him with more desire.

"But didn't you have to work today ?" - I ask as we take a seat at a table outside the cozy restaurant.
I look around, realizing how crowded this area is, even more than the hospital district. Many go to work at this hour, which makes me suddenly feel useless.
I would like to stay in the hospital canteen right now, chatting with my colleagues or a patient while I drink a hot cup of macchiato.
«In an hour.» - he looks at his watch, and then draws the waiter's attention with one hand.
"Thanks for the surprise!" - I remember thanking him. At least now I know he likes museums.
"Nothing. I've been there three times with my pupils, but I love this museum more than the others. " «I understand you .» - I hide the boredom that I felt in there with an obvious and sure tone.

"Your order?" -the waiter forces me to take my eyes off Luois'. "Do you still serve the strawberry cake ?" - he asks smiling.
The boy just nods.
«Bring two slices.» - he winks at me, but, before the waiter can be dismissed, I add: «Even a croissant.» - I raise my index finger.
"Bring two croissants." -
Louis laughs, though I don't understand why. I shrug, starting to spy on the people around me.
"How are Cip and Ciop doing ?" - indicates my belly.
"They make me sleep more. And throw up so much. »- I rest my elbow on the table. "Have you already bought something for them?"

I just nod, while he shows a
grimace of tenderness: "I
only bought clothes, but I
keep them hidden." «When
are you going to tell him?»
- he asks doubtfully.

«He will notice sooner or later.» - he adds
immediately after, fearing my reaction. I lower
my eyes to look at my feet:
"I do not know...
Stay with your sister. »- I say in a low voice, but I jerk my
head up when his hand reaches mine.
I immediately dismiss her, slightly embarrassed, but she
doesn't seem to notice my reaction: «I apologize again for
yesterday evening. You suffered many things in one
evening. "
He is right. Yesterday's dinner could not have been worse, but
it was last night that I understood that I must forget Alex once
and for all.

"Quiet. It is gone. »- I take advantage of the arrival of the
cakes to avoid the speech, so I devour everything I find on the
plate, and I would be intent on licking the cream from the
plate, as good as it is, if it were not for the presence of Louis.

"You have to go to work in a little while. I won't hold you back
yet. »- I stand up reluctantly, then head quickly to the cash
register.
Before Louis can join me, I ask the cashier for the bill and
order some treats to take home. « I'll pay !» - he takes the
wallet from his pocket and starts to ask for the bill, but I
interrupt it:
«I already have.» - I inform him while I turn on his heels,
without seeing his expression, and I

walk away with a box in my hand.

«You did n't have to.» - we go slowly to the car, but I avoid his question.
«I haven't asked you lately ... How is Juliet doing at school?» - I remember the little girl and her ambiguous behavior.
"Actually he's been socializing more lately, but he's dating a boy ..."
"They got together, at least he convinced her not to go away."
- I say more to myself than to Luois, who looks at me confused.
"Like?"
I shake my head, suggesting he let it go as we get into the car.

He gives me directions to go back to school, given my bad sense of orientation, but, after almost a quarter of an hour, we are in front of the building.
«Thanks again!» - I exclaim before he can get out of the car, but he rolls his eyes: «Stop thanking me! It was a pleasure." I smile at his kindness:
"Until next time." - I raise my chin, and then reverse.
The smell of pastries fills my nostrils, which makes me accelerate slightly and can't wait to go home.

The only thing that worries me is the possibility of not finding the empty house, but something tells me that Alex won't be there, not after the last words I addressed to him last night.
It is true that Clara no longer exists for him! For him I will become another woman, one who does not know kindness, who does not listen to him, who neglects him ...
I will make him feel what he made me feel.

I promise myself several times to change my attitude towards him, because I know that every time I see him he will remind me of who we were.
And I know it will be difficult, I am afraid of not being able to and of being trapped in the past for what I feel for him and of not being able to go on.

I take the box in one hand and the bag in the other, and then go to the courtyard, but I stop after my steps when I notice the presence of Alex's car.
Forget it!
I roll my eyes and snort, imagining what awaits me within these walls.

«By continuing to look at the door, you will not be able to open it.» - at first I think it is the voice of my conscience, but then I realize that the voice is all too familiar and hoarse, so I snap my head to my right, finding Alex leaning against the wall near the rocking chair.
I take a step back, opening my eyes wide, then I look around, thinking about how unlikely it is to turn to me in that tone, but I convince myself when it raises an eyebrow, with an amused expression, continuing to look at me.

I look at him, at the same time amazed at his attitude: it seems that he is pretending nothing, that everything he has done to me has no weight.
I enter the house, closing the door behind me, but it is opened immediately afterwards as I approach the sofa, and then sit cross-legged.
I pretend to be uninterested in every movement of Alex, but I end up spying on him sideways, while I open the box and turn on the television.

I take a seat at my side, so close that my leg touches his,
while he moves it up and down nervously: as soon as I
notice his gesture I shiver, but I move immediately,
taking a seat on the opposite side of the sofa.
"I swear I'm not plagued." - the amused tone of his
hoarse voice makes me grit my teeth. What game are
you playing? - I would like to ask him.
"In fact, you're a psychopath." - I whisper, and then regret
having responded to his provocation. Finally I find the courage
to look him straight in the eyes, to notice that he has a corner
of his mouth raised while he stretches his hands at shoulder
height, resting them on the back.

He does not reply, which helps me to understand that he is
not drunk, but his behavior worries me: he is taking me by
the bottoms as until a few weeks ago, so I have to react, I
cannot allow him to have fun with me; after all he has
already had enough fun.
I wear a passion fruit mini cupcake on my lips, and then leave
it between my lips as I adjust the pillow with one hand and
look for the remote control with the other.

"In fact I'm crazy!" - with a quick step I find him astride my
body, while forcing me to lie down
I open my eyes wide and would like to scream them away,
but the sweetness between my teeth prevents me, so I try
to send it away by placing the palms of my hands on its
chest, but it grabs both my wrists and locks my hands on
the sides of my head. I moan angrily to formulate a word in
vain and she realizes it: «I'm not understanding you, it's the
fault of this pastry.
Wait, I'll help you . »- I furrow my now furious forehead, while
her intimacy pushes against mine and her fingers intersect
with those of my hand.
I don't understand his intentions until he lowers himself on my
face and brings his mouth to the sweet between my teeth ..

I open my eyes again when I part my lips, opening them around the cupcake.
It stays attached to my mouth longer than it should, while every muscle in my body stiffens and a strong desire ignites my belly.
I feel her teeth caress the softness of my lips as she takes the pastry, then opens her eyes and looks at me mercilessly.
Chew with a relaxed expression what was in my mouth two seconds ago, and then pass your tongue between your lips:
"You were saying?"

C
h
a
p
t
e
r

3
4

"Move away! KEEP IT! »- I scream annoyed by his behavior.
I push him away from my body, but since this does nothing but amuse him, I decide to change my place.
I take the box with the sweets and go furiously towards my room, but it stops me with my steps when I hear her light laugh:
«You won't play with me anymore !» - I scowl, looking at him intently. I say it more to myself than to him: I don't understand what he thinks of combining, but whatever he has in mind, I will ruin his plan.
«I do what I consider necessary.» - shrugs, but there seems to be no hatred in his voice. I close my eyes:
what I consider necessary ...
What would you like me to believe?

Do you think
it necessary
to pretend
that it is not
over
between us?
What kind of
reasoning is
it?

Whether it's a game or really freaked out, what
worries me is the fact that I can't let him see me weak

«Then go to her.» - I say in a low voice. tilting his head, and
planted his feet on the ground to see his reaction.
I don't know if I will ever get used to the idea of Alex and
Catherine together, as they exchange saliva before my eyes.
I mentally shake my head after that image
shows up in my thoughts. "I prefer to watch
television."
«A little while ago you weren't watching television.» - I
whisper to myself and I know she heard me, but she
pretends nothing happens, while I head towards the kitchen
and I think to start preparing lunch to distract myself from
Alex's presence in the living room.

*I miss you. It's strange not to see you running through the
corridors. * - as soon as my phone marks the arrival of the
message from John, I feel my heart breaking into a thousand
pieces reading it, so without thinking twice I send it:
* Would you like to accompany me to the gynecologist this
afternoon? *

I bite the inside of the cheek, already knowing his answer and
I force myself not to repent.
I would have liked to spend an important moment like this
alone: with the excuse of yesterday's slip I want to spy on the
twins, I can't wait to see how they move, but above all I want
to hear the beat of their little heart. At the thought of it, I get
goosebumps.
* Sure! * - his answer makes me even more anxious: John is
my best friend and he knew about yesterday's dinner. Surely
he will ask me about the progress of the evening and I will be
forced to tell him what happened.

I abandon the phone on the kitchen counter, and then think
about what to cook.
I would have liked a nice seafood risotto, but Giulietta hates
rice, so I opt for a simple fried Michigan pasty and Corndog,
as Giulietta likes ... and the plums inside my belly.
American meals have become once again my favorites, due to the too fat
that characterizes them.

I go looking for meat and potatoes, while I look beyond the
kitchen every so often.
He attached himself to my lips without being able to push him
away earlier: I felt paralyzed under his body and I go back to
frightening myself that the scene a little while ago could repeat
itself.

I watch him get up from the corner of his eye, then I pretend
nothing and I pray to all the gods of heaven that he will not
come in my direction, but my prayers are not heard and the
sound of his steps gets closer, making me understand that is
behind me.
Most likely he sits on the stool on the opposite side of the
island, in his usual domineering posture, while his gaze burns
behind me.

I squeeze the spoon between my fingers and I feel a sudden desire to throw it at him: he must go if he does not want to find a split forehead.

I snort loudly, still annoyed by his presence after a quarter of an hour, and then turn impatiently, ready to scream at him to disappear from the kitchen, indeed, from the house, indeed, from Australia and my life!
But as soon as I turn around, I turn white in the face when I find him with my phone in my hand and a frown. My heart rises in my throat, thinking about the probability that I read the messages between me and John, in which I explicitly speak about my pregnancy.
The spoon falls out of my hand, which causes him to lift his head as he clamps his jaw.

I close my eyes and wait for the worst reaction on his part: I have hidden from him that in six months he will become the father of two babies!
In a split second I regret not saying anything to him and start thinking about the consequences of my action.
His expression is severe, as it has often been lately: maybe he thinks that I don't want there to be a relationship between him and the twins, so I go forward towards him, raising a hand to make me listen, but as soon as I do the first step, my eyes mist up and i can't see anything anymore. I try to find a base, but after a while I also lose strength and meet the cold floor. "Fuck!" - I hear him say, while his footsteps are the last noise I can hear.

The moment is bitter when one realizes that he cannot go back in time and correct an error: I could do it, I would change many things, including certainly the day when I decided to return to the Bronx from Italy. I saw Alex after a long time that same day: he was taller, more attractive, more rude, a mile away from me compared to the friendly relationship that bound us as children.

But I loved him this way from the first day I heard him say bad words to his father, even though I

hated rude people and those who don't respect their parents.

I loved him enough to believe that he felt the same for me.

So much to give him the opportunity to be my first in

everything: the first boy, first love, first physical contact, first sexual experience ... first father of my future children.

And I have always worked hard to make him understand how important it is for me, but I have not had the courage and the will to tell him that we will share twins.

«Baby ...» - I hear whispering over my head, while with difficulty I try to open my eyelids, and then close them again when the light around me appears too strong.

After a state of disturbance, I look around, as if it were the first time that I am inside my own house.

I recover immediately and open my eyes at the exact moment when I meet Alex's confused gaze.

I realize I'm on the sofa, but I remember well the moment when I passed out, after seeing him rummaging in my phone:

"Can you explain what the fuck is wrong with you? Vomit and pass out every half hour! »- utters the words with such sweetness that makes me shiver.

He is bent on his knees on the floor, while his fingers are sneaking through my hair and caressing my chin with my thumb.

They put his hand away and I sit

with one hand on my head:

"Where's my phone?" - I ask in a

low voice.

All this kindness on his part seems strange to me after discovering my secret.
«Ah, yes ... We two must talk.» - I stay in that position and try with all my strength not to turn around to see his expression, while the tone of his voice returns to being cold.
I close my eyes again, hoping to pass out again so as not to face this situation waiting for it to continue:
"Why did you change the password on the phone?" - he finally asks , making my eyes widen when I realize and his words.
I take on an angry grimace, turning to his side: he made me go through hell for the simple reason of not being able to access my phone!
"Is there anything I shouldn't know about you?" - she starts to approach my body with a frown on her face, but I don't allow her to take a step forward and I stand up.
«You don't have to know anything about me.» - I say between my teeth, trying to transmit the hatred I feel towards him at this moment, to then reach him and take the phone from him.
«That's what you say .» - grab my elbow as soon as I try to overtake him, even if his words don't sound like a threat.

I roll my eyes and move away from her body to finish my Michigan Pasty, pending the arrival of Juliet.
I don't want to spend an extra second alone with Alex under one roof.
I can no longer throw up when he is around, otherwise he will really start to think and understand that I am hiding something from him.
But I have to be the one to tell her, otherwise I can imagine her reaction.

«Here I am!» - Juliet's voice fills the hall, so I hurry to sit at the table, as she approaches. «What a good smell! Where are the corndogs? »- when it comes to food, it has a more developed sense of smell than German shepherds.
«Yes, help me to prepare.» - I ask her to follow me into the kitchen, while Alex approaches and sits at the table. I had

hoped for him to leave before lunch, but I cannot avoid
adding another dish, even if I would willingly let him starve.
«How many dishes?» - Juliet's voice forces me to
look at her, but I don't answer immediately. We
have not sat all three at the table for a long time, as
in the old days. I don't want to go back to those
days, but I can't even get out of this situation:
«Three.» - I say with a surrendered tone, while she
smiles secretly.

I look at my watch to see how long I still have before I go to
the hospital, then take a seat next to Juliet, while Alex serves
himself as usual.
"Are you all right at school?" - as I ask the question, the lie she
told Louis comes to mind, so I put my elbows on the table and
look at her curiously:
«Well.» - shrugs quietly, while I think if it is appropriate to
speak of his teacher in front of Alex.

From the first day he saw him sitting next to me, Alex hated
him, as if he expected what really happened, our approach,
and not just as friends.
I too have noticed Louis' strange attitude towards me lately,
and, to tell the truth, he scares me: he is an exemplary, polite,
kind, honest and beautiful boy, but I don't want to disappoint
him because I know that forgetting Alex will not be easy ,
especially when he is still convinced that he can keep me
drooling after him.
After a bit of a struggle between me and me, I come to the
conclusion that it is better to blame him that I am moving
forward, even if it would not be entirely true:
«Why did you tell Louis that I like museums?» - I do n't know
what reaction strikes me the most: Juliet chokes on food and
opens her eyes wide, while Alex jerks her head towards me
and takes on a confused expression .
I watch him sideways closely following the conversation,
stopping the fork in mid-air.

Juliet's amazement turns into a laugh that she tries to hold
back, while I glare at her and I don't think twice before opening
my mouth again:
«Because of you this morning I suffered for three hours ...» - beginning, but
Alex's voice interrupts me:
"You spent time with Louis." - he analyzes, clenching his jaw,
while his eyes remain glued to mine.

I think of the answer to give him, not because he doesn't know
what to say right now, on the contrary, I am spoiled for choice
to make him understand that I am free to do what he has done
with Catherine.
«Should I ask you for permission?» - I raise an eyebrow,
annoyed by the authoritarian tone that he had the courage to
use towards me.
I am clearly taking advantage of his behavior this morning: I had
planned not to speak to him for the rest of my life, but he surprised
me once again.
He keeps staring at me, almost thinking about what to say,
while Giulietta intervenes:
«Michigan Pasty is excellent, you have to try it ...» - he says,
but neither of us looks away.

«You will never meet him again.» - his words sound like an
order, while I notice that he has lost the pride and the
cheekiness of a moment ago.
«I do what I want. I have never stopped you from
going out with Catherine. »- I continue to provoke him,
while he squeezes the glass between his fingers. "Are
you going out with Catherine?" - Giulietta intervenes
again, but I still don't listen to her. "You have no idea
what ..." - Alex starts to say, but I interrupt him:

«I know what I'm saying, and I repeat: don't do my business
anymore .» - I spell out every word well, but its grimace
doesn't change, even if this time it remains silent.
" Did you split up?" - Juliet 's eyes widen and this time I can't
help myself :
"Yes!" - I scream, realizing my conviction when it's too late.

After my words silence reigns: I stop breathing until the moment I
feel the air fail, while Alex does not lose eye contact with mine.
I don't understand what he wants to tell me with those puppy
eyes abandoned by his mother, but it's the first time I've seen
him so serious and thoughtful.
We both know it was obvious, that there is nothing between
him and me just because of him, but admitting it out loud is a
big step forward.
In fact, we've done nothing but avoid or insult each other since
the day I found out who Catherine really was.
We never reproached ourselves to leave behind all that we
have experienced, but that only matters to me.

Now I spit reality in my face, I pulled a nice slap that woke me
up from that state of coma in which I was.

«I have to go.» - I say firmly, biting the inside of the cheek.
I walk away from the table leaving both of them in an icy
position, but it is difficult for me to understand how what I just
said can hurt Alex.
He had the courage to replace them without even realizing it,
giving me the perfect demonstration that I am worth nothing to
him.

I am heading for the hospital, already late: John will surely
be waiting for me angry, since he is fixed on time.
I envy him a lot right now, for the simple fact that I feel
useless, but also because it annoys me the idea of
being replaced at work.

I try to drive Juliet's disappointed expression out of my head after leaving her alone with Alex, while I park next to my friend's car.
"I thought the twins would make you less late."

«Instead it's the opposite.» - I snort as I get out of the car and reach it. «Are you already tired of it?» - pretends to be perplexed while I roll my eyes. "They are not the problem, but the people around me."
«Hashtag Alex ...» - he lowers his head, understanding my problem before I tell him about it.

«He got engaged to Catherine.» - I say suddenly, closing both eyes for the effect that this statement still has on me. John doesn't say a word, but stops a few steps back. "He did what?!" - his expression is more serious than he had the day before his wedding, as he opens his eyelids wide.
«You could have called me, I would have come to you! I can imagine what you went through ... »- he reflects aloud. "Did he tell you?"
«No, I found out at dinner from the primary.» - I explain with a whisper, as images of that scene repeat themselves in my mind and John brings a hand to his mouth, almost thinking of how to help me.
"You have to tell him you're pregnant! That bitch is taking it from you! »- she exclaims, while the doctors turn on our side, making me realize that I am in the corridor on the first floor.
"All the more reason I won't tell him I'm pregnant!" - reading the name of the gynecologist next to the door, I decide to knock.
"You can't keep it from him forever."

"I know, but this ... is not the right time ." - I have time to say
before a woman in a blue coat does not come to open the
door.
John gives me one last look of understanding and then
leaves a kiss on my forehead. «Okay, don't think about it
now and enjoy the moment.» - she winks at me, while the
doctor invites us to enter with the usual grimace that
characterizes the doctors' face.

«You can take a seat.» - he points to the bed next to the
stationary machine, while he turns on a big monitor. «Give me
your hand!» - John jumps on the spot, even more excited than
me, while his eyes light up and reach out to my body stretched
out.
As I reach his fingers, I notice the tremor of my arm, which my
friend reduces by grasping my hand with force.
"How did the first two months go?" - she asks, as she
continues to turn her back. «I didn't realize I was
pregnant, in fact I had a menstrual loss the first month
...
Do I have to worry?! »- I get up half-way up, slightly
frightened, even if it hasn't started to spread the gel on my
belly yet.
«No, no.» - he laughs slightly - «It is a natural wound of the
endometrium. Now let's see if the fetus is healthy. »- raises
my sweatshirt to the base of the breast, while I start to stare at
the screen.
The cold of the gel forces me to grit my teeth, but I don't take
my eyes off the lens:
«I try to find a beautiful pose ... Here it is!» - I put my fingernails in John's
skin as he begins to exalt.

As soon as my eyes end up on the small immobile arms, I neglect
the two who keep talking: I am in another reality, where only my
children and I exist.

I reach out to the distant monitor, wanting to caress them as if they are in my arms right now, while I let out a silent sob.

How did it occur to me to abandon them?

«Cabbages, there are two!» - the gynecologist shows surprise congratulating them for their health, which helps me to start breathing normally.
He starts to push the point away, but I stop her wrist with one hand, almost frightening her:

«Can I look at them a little more?» - I plead with her eyes, while she nods firmly.

I had even forgotten John's presence by my side:
"They are wonderful. Imagine yourself in a couple of months ... »- I close my eyes to his words, while he continues -« ... with a baby in his arm, while you swing him to make him sleep. »- I smile at that scene, but then frown:
"And the other?"
«You are sitting on the sofa in your home: it is raining a lot outside, but you are in front of the fireplace. You have a son in your arms, while the other plays with Alex on the carpet ... »- as soon as I hear his name, a trail of shivers runs all over my body, then I snap my eyes open and let go of his hand.
He rolls his eyes while I assume a melancholy expression: the dream that made me live John would have come true, if Alex had ever loved me.

«Before you go you have to sign some documents. From now on I will take care of you. »- I nod to the words of the gynecologist, who intervenes clearing his throat.

«This, however, is the list of the first exams.» - he hands me a
sheet with several exams on it, including some of which I have
never heard of:

c
o
m
p
l
e
t
e

b
l
o
o
d

t
e
s
t

,

r
u
b
e
o
-
t
e
s
t

,

t

oxotest, Australia antigen research, W

asserman reaction, blood type, comple

t
e

u
r
i
n
e

t
e
s
t

.

I leave the studio with the image of the twins in mind, while John follows me and accompanies me to the car. I would never have understood the emotion of a woman in front of two plums two centimeters long and 2 grams in weight if I were not in these conditions.
I bite my lower lip as I drive to the house which I left angry a few hours ago.
After what I have just experienced and after such intense emotions I would just like to meditate in solitude: I have almost tried what it means to love a child and I would not want to ruin this day.
When I put the key in the door lock, I express the usual desire not to find it inside, but as soon as I open the door, not only did Alex not go away, but he is also in the company of two very familiar women:

"Mum?!"

C
h
a
p
t
e
r

3
5

I remain with my mouth wide open when I meet the figures of my mother and Clelia sitting in front of Alex who, unlike me, seems quite amused, while looking at me attentively.

I whiten my face, immediately thinking of the consequences of their visit: my mother will know the truth and drag me to America with her!
He will surely notice the pregnancy and I can imagine his reaction ...
Now it is clear to me the attitude of my father in yesterday's call: I look again at Alex, while his expression changes, noting my concern.

It is obvious that their arrival was planned by my mother, who did not believe my words when I try to convince her that everything is fine between me and Alex.

And it is she who I look intensely, as if my gaze could help me make her disappear from this house.

After all, I am not surprised to find her in front of me, knowing her: my mother has always intruded and has always done her own thing, which has never bothered me because I realize

that she does it for my good and to make me respect Catholic
morality .
But his coming scares me, like the innocent look that he gives
me right now.

My feet move towards them without my realizing it and I
embrace my mother, after her gaze has softened.
«My daughter, how much I missed you ...» - the tone of her
voice is so fake that I try with all my strength not to raise my
eyes to heaven.
I'm sure I really missed my mother, but her intentions are
different, and she certainly didn't take the plane to come to
Australia just to see me.

"I missed you too, you didn't tell me anything." - I take her
back with a toothy smile, and then turn to Alex's mother, who
seems more serious and sincere than mine.
«Clelia, I am happy with your visit.» - she wraps her arms
around my neck in an elegant way, while I caress her back.
«Thank you, dear.» - he gives me a kiss on the cheek, then
leaves, while my eyes still end up on Alex, who looks at me
with a frown.
It seems to be analyzing the situation to understand the
reason for my discomfort, but then his expression becomes
mischievous as he looks at my mother:
«Take a seat, prepare the coffee.» - I point to the sofa behind me,
and then head towards the kitchen. I breathe out a strong sigh as I
begin to feel a strong heat and lean on the shelf when I see them
start talking to Alex.
My mother is here and I can't lie to her anymore: I have to prepare for the
worst and say goodbye to my life in Sydney.

I turn on the coffee machine and swallow a glass of cold water, and
then return to the three in the living room, to which Giulietta has also
added, who shows her grandmother a notebook to boast of the good
marks.

She looks at me sideways, while I pretend to laugh again and sit between the two women, with Alex in front of her carrying a bottle of beer on her lips.

"I didn't think this city was so beautiful." - my mother takes the floor.

«Tomorrow I will take you for a walk.» - I propose, while Clelia applauds happily, diverting attention from Juliet.

"I haven't visited her for seven years ." - she says and my mother replies.

«At least you have been there, I have never left the Bronx!» - she puts her hand on Clelia's shoulder, while they both laugh.

«I'll show you some nice places ...» - I start to say, but Alex interrupts me with a serious expression. «Let's start from the museums? »He says, without looking at me, but I understand the meaning hidden behind his words. At first I insult him mentally, but then an idea that could really get me out of this disaster comes to mind.

I bite my lower lip and, before I can regret it, I go to the armchair where Alex is sitting. He rests his gaze on my figure, with an interrogative expression, when I sit on his knees: «As you wish, love.» - I lower my eyes and cross his: to say that he is amazed is an understatement, while he remains with beer at midair.

«What ...?» - he begins, but I don't let him continue with the fear that something may come out of his mouth that will ruin my plan.

I push my lips against his cheek, trying not to get caught up in emotions and to think about the fact that I only do it so that my mother and Clelia can look at us.

I feel his chest rise as it fills with air, touching mine, and then feel his hand resting on my knee. It gets even closer, as my

heart starts to beat wildly and the light beard stings the skin of
my lips.
It takes me a while to forget the presence of women in front
of us, but Juliet clears her throat, so I immediately get up,
leaving Alex still perplexed.
«The coffee will be ready.» - I take my eyes off Alex's, looking
out of the corner of my eye at my mother and Clelia looking at
each other.

I literally run into the kitchen and turn off the machine, while I put a
hand on my forehead, but as soon as I bring the cups on the pot
and start to turn around, Alex appears behind me.
The only hope I have left is to make my mother believe what I
insisted on when we spoke on the phone: romantic words and
hugs with Alex will suffice, hide my swollen belly and I will be
able to convince her to stay in Australia.
I jump in Alex's presence, but I avoid his mischievous look as
he crosses his arms and leans on my side.
«I have to help you ... love?» - raises an eyebrow, and
then dangerously approaches my face. I suddenly go
away with the pot in my hand, risking to make him fall at
my feet.
"Stop that! Take off that smile! »- I spit, giving him a grim look.
«Er ...» - nods to my words, not offended at all. He
approaches my figure, taking a strand of my hair between his
fingers as I look at him with a grimace - "Maybe it's better if I
go back to them and tell the truth." - He shrugs his
shoulders, but I widen my eyes and, as soon as he starts to
leave, turning his back on me, I run after him and take him
by the elbow.
"No! Stop, stop ... »- I whisper, drawing his attention and forcing him
to turn on my side. "Why should I do you a favor?" - he asks and
those words are enough to make my blood boil in my veins.

«It is the minimum for how much you make me suffer!» - I
say suddenly, without connecting my brain to my mouth
and almost repenting immediately after.

I don't want him to pity me, I don't want him to look at me like he's really sorry for everything he's done with Catherine.

The smile dies on his lips and of the arrogance of a little while ago no sign remains on his face. He clasps his fingers in two fists at his sides and lowers his head, taking on a thoughtful expression. What are you thinking about? Why do you seem so tormented?

I would really like to ask the first questions that come to my mind, because I don't understand the reason for his insistence: the idea that he is still interested in me makes room in my head, but I immediately delete this hypothesis from my mind and I conclude that most likely it is a

further grip for the bottoms on his part.

He meets my eyes for a thousandth of a second, then turns his back again and walks into the living room. I close my eyes strongly, mentally slapping myself: maybe I ruined everything for two words that I could avoid.

I hold the pot in my hands, as I force myself to go back to them discouraged.

"You don't know how long it took me to convince your father!" - Clelia turns to Juliet, who laughs innocently, while my mother looks at me suspiciously, with a look that heralds a bad conversation.
But before I can say anything, I start:
«How was the trip?» - I ask, pretending to be serene again, even if I can't completely do it and I look out of the corner of my eye, still with a frown.

"It was tiring, actually. I will never take the plane again! »-
my mother's dialect makes Juliet laugh again, who seems
to be in seventh heaven. At least someone is happy with
my mother's arrival.
«We hope we haven't disturbed you ... we wanted to surprise
you and spend a few days with you.» - the grace in Clelia's
voice makes me understand once again how different she and
my mother are, but I have to say that the latter was better able
to educate her daughter, because, unlike Alex, I would never
be able, on my own initiative, to blow up a relationship that
lasted for years.
«No, on the contrary!» - I hasten to reply: surely he will have
understood that something is wrong, perhaps because I am
very bad at pretending.
«It's a beautiful surprise, believe me, but it's a difficult period
.» - I admit and I give up, realizing how crazy my plan has
been.
"Why? Do you have any problems? »- my mother intrudes,
as she closes her eyes, and brings her gaze between me
and Alex.
As if he hadn't really doubted anything, he turns to Clelia, who,
however, maintains a serious expression and a rigid posture.
«Er ... yes.» - I affirm closing my eyes, while I mentally curse
Alex who has not endured me even this time: my mother
opens her eyes wide, slightly approaching her torso and
inciting me to spit the toad, but then she speaks again at my
place:

"I knew there was something behind it.
Alex, I expected to find a ring around my daughter's finger ! »-
now she is looking at him badly, while I whiten my face and try
to catch Alex's reaction sideways.
He just brings beer to his lips as he looks down.
One of the first discussions with Alex is repeated in my mind, in which he
explicitly made me understand that he would never want to marry me, or
have a family with me.

Maybe from there I should have understood that the problem was not me,
but that there was a woman behind it.
But at that time I never imagined that the man I was in love
with would spend his time with Catherine when she came
home late from 'work'.
I don't know what Clelia would think if she knew that her son
had engaged to a spoiled woman like Catherine. Alex does not
respond to his provocation and, after moments of awkward
silence, I decide to continue with a trembling voice:

«I know you won't like what I say ...» - I turn directly to her,
and then continue: «... and I will surely be forced to return to
America with you.» - at my words Alex suddenly raises his
head , but I avoid his reaction.

It was the end that I expected and feared, but perhaps it will
do me good to live away from Alex and Catherine: I lie to
myself thinking I can pretend nothing happens, when in reality
I devour myself inside the thought that Alex and Catherine are
together.
In America I will make new friends and look for a new job, I will
have the opportunity to start my life all over again, which is not
new to me, since it is the fourth time I do it.
"Then? What is this problem? »- my mother's insistence
annoys me, so I try to tell her the truth, but Alex's calm voice
interrupts me:

"We have a wedding to organize."

«What?» - Clelia takes the floor this time looking at my
mother out of the corner of her eye, while the other opens
her eyes at first, then smiles slightly. But Alex's eyes end
up on my figure regardless of their reaction.

It takes me a while to realize his words and chew them: I take
my tongue between my teeth so as not to shout at him, but my
eyes mist up regardless of all the forces I use because they
don't come out.
He can't have really said that! Three months ago he spat in
my face not to see me as his wife, while now he forces me
to endure such a farce in front of my mother.
He is a hypocrite!
He does not know what he says and realizes too late how
bad his words are: he got engaged to Catherine and the
real marriage will not be between me and him, but between
the two of them ...

As soon as he realizes my state he stops the bottle
again in mid-air, to concentrate on my expression, while
I would like to blame him for how much I hate him right
now.

He closes his eyes, then suddenly turns his head towards his
mother, smiling at her and replying to his wishes.
At one time his words, said at another time and other
circumstances, would have made me the happiest woman in
the world, but he managed to speak of marriage only for a lie.

«Why shouldn't I like it? It's beautiful news ! »- my mother gets
up to congratulate both me and the man sitting in front of us
and whose face I don't want to see for the rest of my life.
«Have you already fixed a date?» - Clelia insists, turning to
me, while Juliet at her side seems to be lost.
I just shake my head, but after
a while I find the courage to
speak: "We are both full of
work ..."
«We will help you, don't worry. Clelia and I can organize
everything ... »

«Mum.» - I roll my eyes for her enthusiasm: the smile dies
on her lips noticing my expression, but I continue to relax
her:
«I would like to participate too.» - I say in an obvious tone,
while she laughs and I devise a plan to blow everything up,
unless Alex has already thought about it before pulling out his
great idea.

«Of course, my daughter! The important thing is that sooner or
later you will become a husband and wife. Your father has
been pestering you for centuries! »- he reminds me aloud,
while I would like to scream not to talk so much, since Alex
now looks at me with narrowed eyes.

"I'm hungry. Let's go prepare dinner. »- Alex speaks, while
Clelia congratulates her son who even helps to cook.
If only she knew that Alex only went into the kitchen to fight
with me or take a beer from the refrigerator, she wouldn't be
so happy.
I follow him slowly, formulating sentences to offend him
enough:
"What does your father have to do with all this?" - he asks, as
he leans beside the kitchen oven with a raised eyebrow.
I don't answer him, ready to ask another question, but he
anticipates me;
«He wanted us to get married.» - he answers himself,
almost blaming me for not telling him. "As every father
wants for his daughter." - I answer obvious, not
understanding why he opened this speech.

"Why didn't you tell me about it?" - he insists, while I think if I
answer him or not, but I opt to blame him for his brazenness:

"Why? Would you have accepted me as a wife if I had told
you? »- she clamps her jaw to my words and starts to
approach and reply, but I don't give him time to speak:

«How did you come up with saying that we are getting married?!» - I whisper, glancing constantly at the two women in the living room.
"If it weren't for me now you would be packing your bags to return to America!" - he says in a firm tone. «Better to live from the opposite hemisphere, rather than with you under the same roof!» - after weeks of silence, I can finally tell him how I feel, while he laughs bitterly:
"So why do you want to stay in Australia? To fuck you the good master of ... »- he becomes the real Alex again, but I interrupt him:
"I'm not like you, Alex! It was you who betrayed me and replaced me with Catherine! You pushed me into Louis' arms, and do you know what I say?
He deserves me! Because you had me, but then you threw me away as if I were a rag and I will never forgive you ! "- I conclude, depriving myself of all that I managed to hold inside me for too long and managing to make him change his expression: contracts the muscles of the neck, but in the face assumes a pensive grimace.

I leave him in those conditions behind me, going towards the refrigerator, but he doesn't move from there, although I expected to see him go away angry.

Silence falls in the kitchen for the rest of the evening, while I try to distract myself as I prepare dinner and Apex pretends to help me.
«Your mother looks at us, let me do something.» - she whispers, standing beside me, with a severe tone. I force myself not to raise my eyes to heaven and I just offer him some peeled potatoes and a knife:
"Cut into cubes." - I order him, annoyed by his proximity, even if he doesn't reply and starts to torture the vegetables, but he comes immediately interrupted by Clelia's arrival in the kitchen.

«I could even take a picture of you, but your father wouldn't believe it anyway !» - he looks at his son with a proud look, but Alex keeps his usual bored expression, while she continues.

«Leave me alone with my future daughter-in-law?» - she rests
a hand on my shoulder, after approaching, while a trail of
shivers runs down my back to her words.
Without saying anything, Alex leaves the knife and leaves
the kitchen without saying a word or glancing at me, while
her mother continues to stare at me insistently.
I have always seen Clelia as the model of woman to follow,
regardless of the fact that she doesn't find much time for her
children: she is an elegant woman, but at the same time
simple, she is kind, but also authoritarian.

"Do you think Alex is in love with you?"

C
h
a
p
t
e
r

3
6

Do you think Alex is in love with you?

A month ago I would have burst out laughing at
her face: it seemed obvious to me that Alex
loved me. Already the fact that I lived under the
same roof with him convinced me that I was
his.

But now this question only serves to make me understand
and remember how naive I was. I am amazed at his
question, so much so that I remain puzzled for an
indefinite time, not understanding the meaning hidden
behind his words: as soon as he realizes my troubled

expression he puts his hand on my back and tightens his
lips in a thin line.

«It's a tough nut, my son, we both know ...» - he sighs heavily,
while I wonder what my mother and Alex are talking about on
the other side.

Clelia takes the place of her son, helping me prepare dinner,
while I still find myself frozen, analyzing her words: that she
realized the truth?
It did not seem so, given his serenity:
«But it has changed a lot in recent years. Even now I will see
my son ... get married. »- when his voice begins to tremble, I
turn completely to his side.
"You really made me a happy mother ." - she concludes,
while the tears cloud my vision again. I look up to heaven
not to cry: if only he knew I failed too ...
I feel guilty in front of her and her enthusiasm, guilty for the big
lie we told, but above all for not being able to make Alex the
son of her dreams and the man that I wanted to have by my
side throughout the life.
I approach her and, without thinking twice, I tie my arms
around her neck.
«So you move me .» - she whispers, returning the embrace.
«I will become jealous sooner or later.» - I had not noticed the
presence of my mother behind her, who approaches Giulietta
with our figures and both join in this affectionate gesture.

I laugh heartily, thinking about how ridiculous we seem right now,
but also because I finally relax and understand that their coming
could also help me, beyond the plan:
I have felt so alone lately, thinking that I can face a tormenting
period like this without the need for help, but I do nothing but

reduce myself worse from day to day, regardless of the help of
John, who does not stop leaving me alone.

"I'm starving. How long does this hug last? "- Alex raises his
hands at the hips from the salon, annoyed by this little
demonstration of affection, while I roll my eyes:
«Of course ...» - I
sigh, at the same
time as my mother:
« Men!» - followed
in turn by Clelia.
"Insensitive!"
«Jerk!» - Juliet adds in a whisper that fortunately
the mother does not listen. In fact we get together
underneath, trying to prepare the table before nine
in the evening.

***

I don't stare at the ceiling for how long, now, listless to get out
of bed and face this day. For a moment I had forgotten my
mother's presence in Juliet's room, but a few seconds after I
woke up I realized the opposite.
I wear a pillow on my head with the intention of screaming
about the stress I will have to suffer today: they insisted so
much to take a tour to see Sydney, that they did not even ask
us if we had to work or we had other things to do.
Now that my mom is here, I also have to pretend to go to the
hospital, which only adds to my mood.

I throw the pillow on the other empty side of the bed and force myself to
move towards the wardrobe.
My eyes immediately end up on the envelopes containing the
clothes of the twins, so I hurry to hide them better, and then
go in search of a pair of trousers and a wide shirt.
Yesterday was an intense
evening, especially for Alex's

words: We have a wedding to
organize ...
He said it with such serenity that it made me nervous, as if it
were not a delicate topic for both of us.
I couldn't help shivering at his words: if he really wanted to get
married long ago, we would now be a normal family. Me, him,
Juliet ...

Clelia would really be my mother-in-law and I wouldn't
feel bad for lying to her. We would have traveled back
to America in early summer, since a couple of years
have passed since we last spent the holidays in the
Bronx.
The nostalgia for family lunches and dinners in the
mountains makes me lose myself in the memories of the
summers spent in America, when we all gathered
carefree.
After those dinners Alex took me to his room and made me
feel unforgettable emotions, but at the mere memory, I shake
my head and return to a very different reality.
From now on nothing will be the same and I have to find a
solution before my mother really starts organizing a wedding.

I comb my hair quickly, then drop it on my shoulders in soft
waves. Before leaving the mirror, I position myself in profile,
like every morning, and raise my shirt to the height of the
breasts to greet the twins.
«Good morning to you ...» - I stare at my belly smiling, while I
run my hand over it.
Suddenly the door handle goes down and the noise forces me
to lower the sweatshirt quickly, while Juliet's head peeps into
my bedroom.

«We have prepared breakfast!» - he shouts
enthusiastically, then takes me by the hand and drags me
to the living room, where everyone is already at the table,
including Alex. As soon as his sleepy gaze rests on my
figure, I immediately look away to look at the table full of
smoothies and becon omelettes.
"Since when do you wake up so late?" - my mother's way of
saying good morning is not the best. "Good morning! Today
I don't have to work. »- I shoot the first justification that
comes to mind, as I take a seat next to Alex and try to avoid
his questioning look: he knows he works on Thursday, so I
regret not having thought about it before.

«Er, don't you sleep together?» - Clelia forces me to lift my
head from the smoothie, while I close my eyes, only to
understand that it refers to me and to the man at my side, to
whom I give a look of help , opening his eyes wide.
«I fell asleep on the sofa.» - he replies in a serene tone, not
feeling at all under pressure. Clelia raises her chin and seems
to be convinced, so I sigh mentally and start tasting the green
smoothie, while my Alex looks at me strangely, frowning and
getting closer to my face than necessary:
"You always hated pistachio." - looks at the smoothie in my
hands, while I roll my eyes, whispering:
«Now I like it.» - I shrug my shoulders nonchalantly, making him
understand that I have enough questions: it seems that I am
being interrogated early in the morning, so I have to stop looking
different than usual, otherwise Alex's shrewdness would bring
him to doubt my behavior, and the last thing I want is that he
knows that I am pregnant without having told him, and especially
with my mother nearby.

I eat in silence while my mother begins to speak freely about
the news at Tom's villa and Clelia takes the floor.
I get lost in my thoughts, remembering the image of the twins
in my belly, but the more I think about it, the more I regret not
being able to tell those present, even if I bet that everyone's
reaction will make me feel worse than I already feel:

I can imagine Alex's fury, my mother's disappointment and
Clelia's perplexity if they knew what I was hiding.
«Shall we go?» - Juliet gets to her feet, urging my mother to
get up and Clelia to do the same.

I still don't say a word while the girl makes us walk non-stop: I
find myself behind my mother with Alex at my side, while he
plays with the phone.
Ever since we started, that contraption that is now bothering
me has been holding his hand.
The desire to know who he is messaging with goes beyond
the most rational part of me, which suggests that I do my own
business as we cross the Prince Albert Road to enter the
Hyde Park gatehouse: I let him go a step forward without
realizing it, for then get up on tiptoe and try to go beyond the
height of his shoulders to see what he types on the phone, but
I understand that I am too low to do it, so I go back to side by
side and try to spy out of the corner of my eye.

I do not have time to read the sender's name of the
continuous messages that come to him that I realize that Alex
is watching me.
He raises a corner of his mouth, but I immediately look away
and pretend nothing happens, crossing my arms.

"Why is there a giant condom in the middle of the park?" - my
mother and Clelia are perplexed in front of the pink monument.
«A what?» - Juliet approaches the feet of the obelisk and
raises her head upwards, confused, and then continues- «I
thought it was a giant glacier !» - she is disappointed. "It
was wanted for by an AIDS campaign ." - I explain, while
my mother starts taking pictures. It's a condom! Why does it
have to be so interesting for her?

I secretly roll my eyes as I look around and tighten in my
coat: this square seems to be getting colder than other parts
of Sydney, especially now that we are in the middle of winter.

«This must be Archibald's fountain .» - fortunately the
attention shifts from the genital a few meters away, where I
walk, already tired, following Clelia and my mother.
They begin to exchange information about the fountain as if it were
one of the seven wonders of the world, while my eyes end up on
the opposite side of Alex, but as soon as I do, his arm surrounds
my shoulders and squeezes me to his body.

C
h
a
p
t
e
r

3
7

«What are you doing?» - the trembling voice betrays me, while I
raise my head to look him in the eyes. His powerful arm wraps
around my neck as I try to hold my breath so as not to breathe in his
air. "Your mother keeps us under control." - shrugs, but does not
stop smiling at me, which makes me understand that it is not just for
my mother.

I hide the chills and discomfort that causes me to be close, but
above all the nostalgia that makes me feel that unexpected
gesture.
As soon as its scent strikes my nostrils I immediately move
away from its hidden muscles under his sports sweatshirt.

«This doesn't mean you have to hang on to me .» - I harden my expression, making him remember that if I am now closer to him than five meters it is not to be discovered by my mother and Clelia.

But at that exact moment luck is on Alex's side, as my mother turns around with narrowed eyes.

Without thinking twice, I turn to the side of the man at my side and I sling into his arms, sinking my head at the height of the lower part of his wide chest, given his build too high. Out of the corner of my eye I watch my mother take on a serene expression, which reassures me until the moment Alex's fingers sneak into my hair.

I close my eyes for a millisecond, beandomi of that familiar gesture, but then I open my eyes and raise my head, then take it in an angry tone:

«Take your hands away!» - I threaten him , but he just frowns. «If I don't want to?» - raises an eyebrow, fiddling with my chin, which he holds between the index and thumb. "Don't tell me you've changed your mind about me?" If Catherine ... »- I do to continue with an ironic smile, as we advance towards Dead R., following Juliet, but she interrupts me, resting her index finger on the corner of my mouth.

«Don't name it anymore.» - his seems to be more a prayer, rather than an order, while drawing an imaginary line that goes from my mouth to the corner of my eye. I frown at his words: "You will be my future husband! I'm curious to know how your friendship goes with that old woman. The one with the hanging butt . "- I use the same words he used to describe Catherine to me before I knew her. «Shut up.» - she has time to plead, continuing to look at me with an intensity that makes me goosebumps, but Clelia draws our attention, inviting us to choose from the menu.

I take this opportunity to get away from the heat that his body transmitted to me, while he remains still in his place, staring at me with the same pitying gaze, almost wanting to communicate something that hurts him very much, but that he cannot share with anyone.

I pretend nothing and take a seat next to my mother, setting myself the goal of not ordering the whole restaurant, and I do everything to avoid her penetrating gaze.

"We have an important topic to discuss, so let's go straight to the point." - Clelia takes the floor and gives a quick glance at my mother who agrees, almost encouraging her to continue. I close my eyes slightly worried that the wedding speech will open:
"Have you already set the date?" - he says, so I roll my eyes mentally, even if I expected it to be talked about sooner or later.
I shake my head, while Alex speaks:
"We thought for the next month." - I open my eyes to his words.
«But we are too busy with work.» - I clench my teeth and look at him questioningly and angry at the same time.
If I learned to ascertain yesterday's impulsiveness, given that we had no escape, today I really can't understand it.
He and I will not marry, especially now that he is engaged to Catherine: he has made a choice and I will not play the role of that woman, because I would never wish her to pass on what they have made me suffer. «Come on, my daughter! You can always ask for a few days off. »- my mother claps her hands, while Clelia exults.

I bite the inside of the cheek, analyzing the situation in which I come to find myself: because of Alex, not only will my mother not go away before seeing me in white dress, but she will certainly talk about it with dad, making this wedding a serious event .
I whiten my face only at the idea of Alex in front of me in a suit and tie, while holding my trembling hand on the altar of a church.

I don't know whether to burst out laughing at the too absurd scene or to slap him for getting me in trouble.

Regardless of the feelings that still bind me to him, I'm not so blind as to allow him to make fun of me so easily: while he spends the nights on the same bed with Catherine I sleep on an empty and cold bed, and it must be enough to understand that Alex will never be the man I want to have by my side all my life.

He was so selfish that he didn't think of me as he brushed against another woman's skin, and I will act accordingly.

This marriage will not be there, even if it means ruining my reputation as a good woman:
I want a new life here in Sydney without him by my side, and it won't be Alex and my mother to stop me ...

«We have very little time! Have you already chosen the dress? »- Clelia's voice forces me to divert my thoughts and participate in this absurd conversation.
I just shake my head as she opens her eyes wide and Juliet continues to look at me in confusion. "Then it will be our starting point ." - my mother takes the floor.
"You're free tomorrow afternoon, aren't you? You can do tomorrow. »- Alex's voice annoys me so much that I close my eyes and bite my tongue so as not to slap them.

I don't understand what wins from all this: he doesn't want to get married and the fact that he insists so much makes me fear that there is something behind all this.
He is so complex and moody that only now do I realize that I don't really know him: I stare at him insistently, while my mother approves his proposal.

I would like to understand what he is hiding, even if it could be something really bad that would make me feel bad.

Fortunately, the only noise you hear for the following two hours is that of the forks, often interrupted by my mother, then by my pseudo-mother-in-law and Juliet.
Contrary to what I thought yesterday, they are not supporting me at all, on the contrary, now they also come out with a wedding to be organized within a month.

The only thing that would console me in all this mess is perfect solitude, while I find myself in front of the television eating two tubs of ice cream, or reading the books John gave me about pregnancy, or going shopping for the twins of new.
I'm sorry I can't give them the time they deserve.
As soon as I think of John, I pick up the phone to send him a message: he doesn't know that my mother is in town. He doesn't even know about the marriage that Alex brought up, but above all I want to vent my anger with someone, even if not even John would be able to solve my big problem.

* Are you alive? * - sending, while Juliet looks up from the phone:
"There is an atelier a stone's throw from here." - he raises his cell phone, indicating that he has searched for it with Google, while he winks at me.
If you think I'm going to wear a white suit to please you, you're wrong!

I turn my attention away again when John's message arrives, at the same time as one from an unknown user.
I abandon the latter and focus on what I receive from my friend.

*Yes, my patient does not. * - I grimace with displeasure and hurry to answer:

I'm sorry.

*It's past ... Why did you write to me ? * - I can imagine his disappointed expression.

*Can't I have a chat with my best friend? *

*When you write to me you do it to complain about Alex, to

make fun of the models of ANTM, or to askme to lend you my

Wahl to shave your legs. * - I roll my eyes after reading his

words, but then I close the phone when I notice Alex spying

on me out of the corner of my eye, but he immediately shifts

his gaze when he notices that I look at him sideways.

«... so I will take care of the location.» - Clelia turns again to my mother, so I take this opportunity to go back and talk to my friend.

*See you tomorrow morning in the square near the hospital. * - I send, but I don't have time to turn off the phone, sure of my friend's answer, that I get a message quickly.

*If you really insist! * - I frown, but burst out laughing when I notice that I have sent the message to Louis, attracting the attention of those present, especially Alex who clamps his jaw: «It's John, he said he wants to meet you.» - I try to get away, while my mother smiles tenderly and I imitate her:

«Tell him we would have time, since we will be here for the whole month !» - the smile dies on my lips, as we get up from the table to finally go home.

*I got the wrong number, but if you want you can join me and John. * - I send without thinking twice, while we walk slowly.
I like Louis' company: he is a good man, a good
teacher and very kind indeed. It seems he knows
what to say and when to say it.
I dare not imagine how many friends he has for this behavior, but surely there must be many.

He has a big heart, so much so that he took me to a museum only because Juliet said he was a lover of contemporary art.

*I'll be there! Are you all right? * - I frown at his question, but I don't have time to answer that we get home.
Why shouldn't I be fine? By now he has understood that for me Alex is past water.

I take the key from my Pashli as soon as we approach the gate, but I jerk my head up when Alex's voice attracts everyone's attention:

"Catherine ?!"

I grit my teeth only at the sound of his name pronounced by Alex.

«Surprise!» - she raises her arms, coming towards us as if she were doing a fashion show with on her what for me is a sweater for her length, but for her it is a dress that reaches down to her lower back.

He smiles with a fake kindness as he comes towards me, then
he frowns, while I whiten his face, suddenly realizing that it
could ruin everything.

I glance at Alex for help, but he seems more worried than
me, as he stands next to me, in front of the front door of our
house.

**C
h
a
p
t
e
r

3
8**

Catherine approaches my face and greets me with a kiss on
the cheek, while I take on a disgusted and surprised
expression at the same time:
«Hi, Clara!» - she says between her teeth, while I would like to
ask her what she is doing in my courtyard and why she is
treating me as if we were best friends.
I watch his arm lean on my shoulders, while I frown: *if you do not
move away, I will detach your arm and you will be less!*

Surely Alex will have informed her about the arrival of her
mother, but I don't understand why it helps me cover myself: if
she knew that my mother could force me to return to America,
she would be the first to tell her that Alex and I broke up.

I try to look happy with her presence, but the result continues
to be a grimace, while Alex looks at her sideways with her jaw
clenched, as if not expecting her presence. N *on even know to
control your girlfriend!*

«Er, are you ...?» - my mother smiles half as she moves her
gaze between me and Alex, but Catherine doesn't give me
time to answer that she immediately positions herself in front
of my mother:
«I am a friend of Clara, it is a pleasure to meet you.
Alex told me he had an elegant mother, but not so much. »- I roll
my eyes, understanding the reason for his cordiality with my
mother: he mistaken her for Alex's mother for I don't know what
reason.
I look at Alex sideways, but his frustrated expression
makes me understand that he is worse off than me.
«Thank you.» - my mother blushes and shows her teeth,
while Clelia looks at her from head to toe until Catherine
notices her presence.
«Hello.» - she just raises her chin, while I bite the inside cheek so
as not to insult her: she greeted what she thought was my mother
with an air of sufficiency and it is evident that she came to be
noticed by Clelia.

I can't help smiling, almost happy that his plans are not going
as planned.
In fact, Clelia is still perplexed and avoids answering his
words, so I decide to intervene, impatient to see her
expression mortified, but Alex precedes me.
«Er, let me introduce you to my mother.» - she advances
towards her, placing a hand on her bare back and pointing to
Clelia.
I take my eyes away from her hand to be pleased with
Catherine's face: she opens her mouth wide and remains
for an indefinite time, staring at Alex's mother, who does
not move an eyelash and maintains a neutral expression.

«Let's go inside.» - I roll my eyes at her invitation, while
Catherine tries to remedy: «I am mortified ...» - she turns
again to the woman in front of her, but Alex doesn't let her
finish: «Let's go. »- he looks her straight in the eyes to
convince her, while I decide to move and reach the inside of
the house.

The first time I saw her in here I freaked out, but this time I
can't help pretending that her presence not only doesn't
bother me, but I appreciate it.
It 's what she wants, along with Alex, that is, to have my
house, my space, but do not allow them to appropriate
what is mine, even at the cost of supporting Alex every
day.

I go straight to the kitchen and extract the meat from the
freezer, pretending to be busy so as not to spend time in
front of Catherine's slapping face, but then I realize that I am
forced to do it, since that woman introduced herself as a
friend of mine.

I can't believe my mother didn't suspect: Catherine is my
exact opposite, both in physical appearance and in her
behavior, and it's the first time I admit I have virtues.
Someone like you could never be part of my group of
friends.

"You're going to be at my daughter's wedding, are n't you?" -
the first question my mother asks Catherine as soon as I get
close to the sofa, makes me lose a beat again, so I glance
quickly at Alex, who avoids me and look carefully at
Catherine.

His persistent gaze on her body makes me feel a burden on my stomach, but I bring my eyes back to her, fearing her reaction.

I am even more confused by her serene expression, as if she already knew that Alex and I are getting married, or rather pretending to get married.

«I will be the bridesmaid !» - she says enthusiastically, while I do everything not to roll my eyes. «Then you must help us! The wedding has to be organized in a month and we haven't thought about the bridesmaids' dresses. "

«Mom?!» - I ca n't stop myself and interrupt her. It becomes unbearable when he insists on a topic, especially now that he brazenly addresses Catherine, even if he doesn't know who he really is. «What is it?» - frowns , while the eyes of those present suddenly end up on my figure. I mentally slap myself for my impulsiveness and try to remedy:

«It will be a small wedding, let's not exaggerate.» - Catherine is the first to react to my words, rolling her eyes:

«Come on, you're getting married, you're not having a birthday party!» - I clench my teeth again, as I try to understand what is really going on: both she and Alex are insisting on this wedding so as to make me doubt them real intent.

"You know me, I'm not a snob." - I put a hand on his shoulder and press my lips into a hard line. He perceives the irony in my voice, but does not move an eyelash and looks at my hand with a fake smile. «In fact you have to give yourself a wake up call, my friend !» - his gaze hardens, while he turns his back on the two women in front of me, and then continues acid: «Otherwise you risk getting yourself stolen Alex.» - she says and bursts laugh immediately afterwards.

I bite my tongue at first, and then remember that my mother and Clelia are in this living room, so I pretend a laugh for the umpteenth time.

«How dear you are. Come more often! »- my mother exclaims
convinced and I roll my eyes, taking advantage of the fact that
none of them are watching me.

«Of course, you will find me here every day, but now I have to
go.» - he says and stands up, then kisses me on the cheek.
"Don't make that face, you'll see me more often from now on
!" - grabs my cheekbone between the index and middle
fingers, which makes me want to slap her hand, but I can
hold back and greet her in a civilized way , while Alex
intervenes: «I'll take you .» - he says, while I close my eyes.

When Catherine is around Alex she is no longer in herself:
it still costs me to admit it, but ... it seems that she cares
about that woman, and this torments me even more.
He never felt uncomfortable at my side and he wasn't staring
at me in the same way he seems to admire Catherine now
and if before I thought he liked her physically ... now I'm
afraid I feel something for her.

Just at the thought I stop in my place and stop breathing:
"Everything good? You're pale. "- Clelia gets to her feet and
brings me back to reality, so I decide to react and invite her to
take her place again:

"It's fatigue, I'm going to prepare dinner." - I try to make a
toothy smile, but mine end up on Alex and Catherine chatting
at the door.

I go into the kitchen with my head down and lost in thought,
but I immediately withdraw the tears so as not to be caught by
Juliet, who stares at me, sorry.
I wink at her to make her understand that I'm fine, but I can't
smile and I go back to work the pork on the sink.

I suddenly feel bad, even worse than when I discovered Alex's betrayal: I was really put in the background by him in front of Catherine, so much so that for him it seemed that only she existed for how she didn't stop looking at her.
I always knew I was abandoned by Alex, but having the practical demonstration of it destroyed me.
I felt a nullity in front of her, even if I still don't understand what is in her: the last relationship Alex had with a completely redone girl was six years ago, with Chris.
Then I thought he got tired of that type of woman and I started to believe that he was perfect for him, despite our differences.
Thinking about the fact that we are completely opposite, it was a miracle that our relationship lasted so long, but I continued to believe that the love I felt towards her was enough.

I sigh heavily, then approach the dishes, complaining about placing them higher and higher, so I try to stand on tiptoe and reach the shelf.
I snort and do to turn around and take the usual chair, but I don't have time to turn around, that I feel a presence behind me.

I immediately notice that it is Alex, who comes so close that my back adheres perfectly to his chest.
I close my eyes and run my tongue between my lips, while my muscles tighten.
"What do you need?" - puts a hand on my side as he tilts his head and sighs at the hollow of my neck. «The green plate .» - I reply immediately, holding back a groan: I miss her touch so much that I just need a touch on her part to go into fibrillation.
Drag your fingers up slowly, but as soon as I notice that it is approaching my belly, I remember being pregnant and I turn around to face it, while I try to avoid her gaze and the proximity of her mouth.

Without thinking twice and with crazy speed I raise my knee to
hit him in the middle of the legs, and then move slightly away
with a raised eyebrow and not at all repentant.
He groans in pain, but I enjoy in front of that scene, hoping to
have hit him more than he has done until the moment
Catherine was among us.
Slowly raise your head, with one hand on your genitals,
to look at my pleased expression, as I cross my arms
and look at him from above:
"I told you not to play with me." - I have the courage to say
after a while.

«Fuck you ...» - he says between his teeth, but I don't listen to him and I go
back to cooking even in the absence of a dish.

C
h
a
p
t
e
r

3
9

I leave the kitchen very tired, but above all perplexed by the
scene I witnessed today between Alex and Catherine, as I
head towards the sofa, where everyone has already taken a
seat, together with him, while watching Warrior.

As if my gaze on his profile had called him back, he moves his
eyes from Tom Hardy to my figure, which forces me to move
forward and look away again:
"I'm sleepy." - I admit, kissing my mother, then bending close
to Clelia and surrounded the neck by the shoulders.
I finish saying goodbye, giving Juliet another kiss on the
cheek, while I avoid Alex, who is still sulking at having
pulled his knee.
I leave them together to discuss and be moved about the film,
with the exception of him, who continues to use his annoying
contraption.

I close the door behind me and stand in front of the mirror
again, kissing two fingers and then putting them in contact
with my belly:
«Goodnight to you.» - I whisper, tilting my head to see them
better.

I open the closet doors in search of the same pajamas as I did
last night, but finally I am satisfied with a sweatshirt that I
bought for Alex a year ago and I slide it out of my head, without
thinking twice.

I sigh as I throw myself on the blankets, since I lack the
desire to cover myself: I continue to remember perplexed
the depth of Alex's eyes while looking at the blonde
Barbie.
A squeeze in the stomach makes me move on the bed from
one side to another, without however finding peace.
I curse myself for not being able to think of anything else,
when in reality I had planned not to give him the opportunity to
humiliate myself again.

I bring my bare legs up, playing with my fingers to distract
me, but nothing seems to help me, so I decide to close my
eyes and let Morpheus embrace me.

For the first time I agree with John that I have to supply myself
with Barberol tablets to fall asleep peacefully: I sink my lower
lip between my teeth and try to hold back a laugh while I
observe the empty part of the bed.
I don't know where I found the courage to kick them in the
lower parts, but I didn't regret my action, on the contrary ... it
made me feel better, even if for a short moment.
In fact, during the dinner my mother did not stop talking about
confetti, cakes and centerpieces, while Clelia kept her
company and I kept nodding and pretending to be as excited
as they were.
At the mere thought of what I will have to face tomorrow I feel
sick: in the morning I certainly cannot stay at home, otherwise my
mother would understand that I don't work, and fortunately I am in
the company of John and Louis, but I have to find a justification
for the others too days when I should have been to the hospital.

As I get lost in thoughts and try to find a solution, putting my
ideas in order, I hear a noise at the door and I feel it open, so
I pretend to sleep and ask for my eyes, still facing the part of
the bed that, until a month ago, it was occupied by Alex,
therefore with her back to the entrance.

From the step and heavy breathing I understand it's Alex, so I
blush, realizing that I have bare legs, while the sweatshirt
rises up to my hips.
I feel observed, so I bend my legs and bring them close to
my chest, but his voice makes me jump: "It doesn't help." -
I tighten my eyes tightly to his words, while I feel that he
traces every millimeter of my exposed skin with his eyes,
until you get to the pink polka dot panties, which serve to
play down the situation, since there are many 'Fil' printed
on the Hercules cardboard.

«What are you doing in my room ?» - I snort, turning around again, then getting up and positioning myself under the covers, while he continues to stare at my sweatshirt.

"I could not find the pajamas." - I add in a low voice, explaining why I am wearing his sweatshirt while returning to the same position as before.
Avoid my words, to answer the question in a tone of sufficiency.
"My mother asked us why we sleep apart." - I open my eyes to his words, observing Alex's every move, as he approaches the bed, sitting turned away, then takes off his socks.

He puts his long fingers on his belt to get rid of his pants too, so I decide to turn to the other side. Having it on my own bed makes me goosebumps: I don't trust Alex, especially if he is ten centimeters away from his body and with only a pair of underpants on him. I feel the mattress move under its weight, then I reach the far end of its body. I hear him sigh:
«In a while we would be husband and wife.» - he says after a while, but his words do nothing but increase my nervousness.
«We will not get married.» - I say in a firm voice: I will not satisfy Alex and Catherine, since behind all this story there is something that I am completely unaware of.
«Sure.» - he whispers ironically, then I frown and I turn to him.
«What do you have in mind?» - I ask acidly, resting my head on the pillow and looking at him from below with a serious expression.
He shrugs, without losing eye contact with my eyes, but he seems anything but serious, while he puts his hands behind the back of his neck.
"Maybe you don't understand." - I close my eyes trying to threaten him, and then continue: "I'll be the one to prevent it."

His expression becomes more serious than mine, but he does
not respond and continues to look me straight in the eye,
almost making me shiver.
"Why did Catherine help me ?" - I insist, already knowing that I
have no serious answer from her: "She is a good woman." -
Her words only make me nervous again: she defends her and
says that Catherine is a holy, when she had sex with him
while knowing that on the other side there was a woman
waiting for him at home.

I bite the inside of my cheek and go back to the other side,
while Alex laughs slowly. "You are so jealous."
«I 'm not!» - I immediately exclaim : if for Alex Catherine she is
full of virtue, for me she remains a woman without personality
and respect for herself, then I will never be jealous of her and I
don't understand how the man does to my shoulders to go after
her.
In anger, I step out of the blankets, regardless of being half
naked, and then go to the closet and take out two blankets,
feeling her eyes on her, but avoiding him.

Evidently she didn't understand that I'm serious, so I decide to
fall asleep on one blanket on the ground and cover myself
with the other, and then take the pillow from the bed, waiting
for an annoyed reaction from Alex. But all he does is laugh
again, showing the dimples on the sides of his mouth: he gets
up from the bed and reaches me at a padded pace, but I hurry
to occupy all the available space, looking at him badly.

He does not move an eyelash and looks at me mischievously,
as he lowers himself on the ground and climbs over me with
one leg, lying on my body and making me choke on the weight
I have to bear.

«What are you doing?» - I hold my breath, but then brings the torso slightly to the side of my body, continuing to keep the long legs above mine and lacing my chest with one arm. «So you don't run away.» - he whispers on my face, while he looks at me satisfied from above. The heat of his sigh hits me, while my nostrils are affected by the smell of his perfume: I look at him carefully, as if I could manage to get into his head and understand what he feels:

«It is you who run away, not me ...» - I let him embrace me in his own way, but I push him away with my cold tone and with my convinced words.
He assumes a puzzled expression and starts to speak,

but I close my eyes and pretend to fall asleep with my

head at the hollow of his neck, leaving him to stare at me

with that dark and illegible look. ***

"
A

w
e
d
d
i
n
g
?
"

"
Y
o
u

g

e
t

m
a
r
r
i
e
d
?
!
"

John and Louis' faces don't help me find the solution I'm looking for, so I run my hand through my hair and snort loudly. "But you didn't quarrel with Alex because he didn't want to marry you?" - John doesn't abandon the shocked grimace as he turns the spoon in the cup of tea, but I just shrug my shoulders: if I had understood what passes Louis' expression, instead, she is completely thoughtful: she seems to have completely lost herself in her thoughts, as she lowers her head.

«You ... do you want to marry him?» - Louis' question forces me to raise my head and frown.

It is not the first time that I think of the family that I could have formed with Alex: the idea of having a ring excites me a lot and seeing myself in the mirror in a white dress would really be a dream.
I can't lie to myself, saying that it never occurred to me to talk to Alex about it, but I always felt stuck, almost aware that Alex would reject me.
But I never stopped thinking about the moment when my father takes me by the arm and guides me as we walk towards the priest.
At his side are John, Andrew, Justin, Josh and Ash, who nudge themselves and laugh under the mustache, from rascals which have remained.

But Alex, in front of the priest, is serious: he cannot relax
because of the strong love that binds him to me and because he
would like to take me home immediately, rather than waste time
in front of the priest who does nothing but talk. When he looks at
me he seems to forget the outside world until the priest declares
us husband and wife and kisses me with an inappropriate
passion for an Anglican church.

I shake my head and look back at Louis as
he did a little while ago, noting his
perplexity: "Of course not!" - I answer
obvious, and then grab the straw between
his lips.

"Then I'll help you."

C
h
a
p
t
e
r

4
0

«I have to go.» - Louis stands up with an angry grimace on his
face.
I almost regret talking about it in front of him, fearing that he
might really do something, since he's Catherine's brother.
I just say goodbye to him with a wave of my hand and a drawn
smile, while I see him walking away with a fleeting pace.
"What's wrong with him?" - John takes the floor, then returns
to look at me seriously.

«I don't want to go home.» - I admit before I can go
back to talk about what I confessed to him a little while
ago, but he seems to read me in thought:

«Alex would never do it.» - he says confidently, then I roll my
eyes and look him straight in the eyes: «After everything he
has done to me, do you continue to defend him?» - the tone of
my voice sounds angrier than I wanted, so I close my eyes in
a sense of repentance.
I sigh, without apologizing for my anger, but it doesn't
seem to give him much importance, in fact he changes the
subject immediately after:
"If you don't want to go home immediately, you can go to my
house ." - she tilts her head, while I press my lips in a hard line
and nod with conviction.
I prefer to spend a morning with John and Andrew, rather than
undergo my mother's interrogation, especially before choosing
the wedding dress.
We get up, after paying the bill, and we start walking towards
our machines:
«Alex is complex.» - I frown at his words, but this time I decide
not to interrupt him so as not to offend him: «But he is
obviously in love with you, Clara.» - this time I lose a beat and
I feel my hands tremble as much as I have wanted to hear
those words from someone other than my conscience.
On the one hand I think John only says this because he is my best
friend and he wants to make me feel important, but on the other
hand I want to terribly believe him, so I let him continue talking and
remain silent:

"It's just that ... he proves it differently," he shrugs as he drives
to his apartment. «Going to bed with Catherine?» - I laugh
ironically, and then roll my eyes and beg him to stop deluding
me.

"We both
know who
Alex really is
." - I sigh
again,
frustrated by
the topic.
Not only did he not try to deny that he betrayed me, but he
even felt he had done nothing that I should not have expected.

«Come in.» - she urges me to go up the stairs, and then she
starts talking again: «I will accompany you this afternoon, but
if you don't want this wedding, talk to your mother ...»

"Thanks ... if it were that simple ..." - I enter his apartment,
finding Andrew in front of the television. Sometimes I get
scared by the similarity between him and Alex.
«Andrew.» - I give him a smile, while he, as soon as he looks
at me, gets up from the sofa and comes towards me with a
serene expression.
"I haven't seen you for centuries ." - he frowns , hugging me,
and then invites me to take a seat around the living room
table.
I don't speak until the moment I sit on the chair and John joins
us with bowls of ice cream in his hand.
"You can't even get your mother to put your feet on your head.
You are responsible and independent. »- my friend resumed
his speech just now, while I press my lips together.
"You know my mother. If I want to stay here, I have to lie to
her. "
«But don't even get married! And then ... does Catherine
know? »- she insists, then I puff and straighten my back
against the back of the chair.
I nod, then my eyes end on Andrew who stares at me
insistently and confused, as if Alex hadn't told him about his
crazy idea.
"Marriage?" - his question forces me to raise my eyebrows:

"Don't you know?" - I immediately ask : if before I was
worried that Alex had plotted something behind me, now I'm
completely sure.
He always talks to his friend, so much so that Andrew
probably knows him better than me, but he has not told him
such an important thing ...
"Clara, the time has come for you and Alex to solve ..."
"Andrew, don't start." - I raise my head and give him a
knowing look, but that doesn't move him at all and returns to
praise his friend, so I interrupt him:

«I will not be fooled by him again !» - I raise the tone of my
voice, which encourages him to defend Alex again:
"You're exaggerating!" - it's the first time he speaks to me in
such an angry tone of voice, so much so that John takes it
back:
«Andrew, calm down!» - he says between his teeth, but I
avoid him and I keep on venting, as if I was in front of Alex
and I could express the evil he has done me all these months.
"He cheated on me with another woman!"
«He only hid your identity from you!» - he stands up, so I
imitate him:
«He got into his underwear!» - I scream immediately after
his words, waiting for him to reply and continue to support
his best friend, but he takes on a confused expression and
opens his eyes wide, as if he has no idea what he is talking
about .

«Alex has never fucked with Catherine.» - he says confidently, while
his tone of voice lowers and stares at me, almost to understand me.
«Well, apparently he hid a lot of things from you.» - I
shrug, but I try to calm down. Basically it is not his fault
that Alex is a living mess who is a bully by trade.

I abandon her eyes and sink the spoon into the ice cream, taking her seat on the chair again. "Why did you think I was angry?" - I add in a low voice, but replies after quite some time, while John continues not to intrude.
"Because you understood that she was not old." - his explanation makes me frown.
I am not so exaggerated and I am going to say it out loud, but I do not have time to get up again and start walking out of the apartment with a fleecy step.
«Where are you going?» - I ask, but John rests his hand on my arm, making me understand that it is better not to try to stop him, because he will do his own thing. I shrug and turn my attention to John:
«So will you accompany me ?» - I change the subject so as not to start ruining this badly started day.
"I can not miss. I want to see you with a veil. »- she says, and then she finishes eating in silence, strangely. I look at the ice cream indefinitely, until I start to feel nauseous from the annoying smell of dark chocolate.
«I'm going ...» - I point to the bathroom with my thumb, while he rolls his eyes and nods: "This time try to peck the hole in the bidet!" - he shouts from behind me, and fortunately I can fulfill his wish.
The twins start to get naughty before they are even born, let alone later.
I keep wondering what my mother's life will be like, with two children to grow up and a job to do, without a man by my side who can help me at home.
Alex wouldn't have done it regardless, even if I pretended that nothing happened: I can't imagine him as a father or husband.

«Would you like to be a mermaid or a princess?» - John starts to laugh, while he gives me a passage towards the atelier that Juliet proposed: I glare at him and I don't answer his provocation.

In fact, I have always dreamed of a princess dress with three-quarter lace arms and a puffy skirt, the classic dress of dad's good daughter:
I secretly admire Antonio Riva and keep his collections, but I also know that I will never wear one of his clothes.
The experience with Alex made me understand that a man cannot be trusted, even when you think he has eyes only for you, as I deluded myself until recently.

"Are your mother and mother-in-law already there?" - I nod to his question, mind I keep my belly with one hand: I open my eyes and start to tremble from head to toe when I think of the twins:
"And if they notice the pregnancy?" - I raise my voice, while he frowns, then pops his tongue:
«You are only two months old, you can say that you have just eaten and you have a slightly swollen belly, but it is not evident.» - he says firmly and his safety comforts me, while I slightly lift my shirt and look at my belly. Maybe he's right and my belly isn't as swollen as it looks before my eyes.
I shrug and start talking again:
"By the way, park your car in front of a take away." - I affirm, feeling my stomach growl. «I only hope that everything you eat will make the twins fatten and not you.» - he says to himself, knowing that I can listen to him regardless, while he stops the car, as I asked him.

I get out of the car and, having satisfied my digestive system, I follow John to the atelier, in front of the door where I find the two women chatting as if they were old friends. For the way my mother gesticulates, she stands out from the delicacy of Clelia, who remains in rigid posture, as if she had grown up in a royal family.

I laugh under the mustache while my mother surrounds
John with her arms: «Son, you have become such a
handsome man !» - I continue to laugh, looking at John
completely at ease. I leave them behind, while I nod my
head to Clelia to enter the building and conclude as soon
as possible.
«Juliet?» - I look around, realizing his absence.
«She confessed to me that she went out with a boy.» - Clelia
laughs, winking at me, while I nod and turn my eyes back to
the atelier.
If only it were possible to borrow the dress only, rather than
buying it definitively, I wouldn't have to spend as much for a
day that will never come, but something makes me really
want a moment like this, as if everything was real and
wanted by me than from Alex.

I hear my mother's voice, a sign of the fact that
the two of them entered behind us too: "Are you
excited?" - Clelia catches my attention.
«Scared, to be honest.» - I admit, as I look around and I
notice that I am surrounded by girls of my same age, or even
younger, who seem to be in dilemma as to which dress to
choose.
A wise man said that a woman has more difficulty choosing
the dress than the husband she spends the rest of her life
with.
It would have been enough for me to be his ...

«Don't be, it's your day.» - gently caresses my back, while he
turns his eyes on the different clothes. I imitate her and try to
catch the simplest of the wedding dresses present in this
atelier. I approach one entirely in lace and milk-colored, but I
jump when I am joined by a woman: "I saw it first ." - she
screams, then I take two steps back and immediately answer:
«Okay !» - I frown , while my mother comes forward to jump
on her, but I take her by the arm and drag her to the opposite
side of the light room.

I roll my eyes and, even more discouraged than before, I pretend
to go looking for another dress, but my eyes are really captured by
a particular dress, so white that it stands out from the others
around it.

It seems to be the dress dictated by my dreams and my
mother approaches it, looking sideways at me:
«How about this?» - indicates the mannequin who wears the
dress with the bust entirely in lace and the skirt swollen at the
right point, enriched by few details.
A shiver runs through my spine, imagining it on me, but I just
shrug my shoulders in front of my mother, who smiles and
calls an employee.

Shortly after I find myself in a dressing room and a lady
follows me with a hanger in her hand: «I'll help you put it on.» -
she says with an inappropriate monotony, but I avoid her tone
of voice and I get rid of my clothes, remaining half naked in
front of a vertical mirror.

It helps me tie every single bow behind me, while I lose I forget
how you breathe, while I admire my reflection.

I tilt my head and, while the woman continues to speak, I lose
myself and feel my eyes filled with tears in front of that beautiful
reflection: for a moment I delude myself that I am a real bride,
with a dress that wraps me perfectly in every shape and
suddenly makes me fall in love with every imperfection of my
body.

But my illusion doesn't last long when my phone vibrates on a
chair:
«I'll pass it on.» - the employee helps me to grab it, so I open
it to see the arrival of a message. Without even looking at the
sender I understand that it is from Juliet when I read the
content.

* Alex and Catherine have entered your room. I tried to
prevent it ... *

C
h
a
p
t
e
r

4
1
Alex

I have no idea where she is, and especially who she is with
right now, although in theory she should be working at this
hour: I would have followed her if only I hadn't woken up two
hours late, but I just had to pass the night with her so as not to
get angry as soon as I wake up.

I go around the house like a living dead looking for a bottle
with liquid, which has at least a small percentage of alcohol,
taking advantage of my solitude.
As soon as I arrive in the kitchen, however, I frown when I find
Clara's mother and mine sitting opposite each other, while
they chat in the early morning:
"Are you going out?" - I look at them from head to toe with
a raised eyebrow, noting that they are already dressed
and tanned like clowns on their faces.
«Let's go back to see the giant condom .» - my mother-in-law
is so refined that I want to compliment her sometimes, and
ask her why she didn't pass on her character to her daughter.

It took a long time for her to forgive me for telling her daughter
she was adopted, and implicitly, she always declared war on

me to test myself and see if I was the right man for her daughter. After years of annoyance, she gave up, but now her daughter is the one who breaks my cock, especially when I go out with that jerk in a suit and tie.

Maybe she forgot what I'm capable of doing for her, including making Louis her patient: I've been gritting her teeth for quite some time and I've been enduring everything she's been up to lately, but I won't let her get away from me .

I just wanted to make her jealous, but I hadn't considered that Catherine could get mad at me.

I am so blind to Clara that I didn't even realize that the bitch felt anything for me, even though I had clearly told her to pretend my girlfriend to get Clara away from Louis.

But I was screwed because Clara had the opposite reaction and Catherine started blackmailing me: I

shouldn't have confided in her, nobody can trust a woman who doesn't even wear a thong. If Juliet knew she was my daughter, she would never forgive me ... but I don't want to lose her.

As much as I made her suffer from an early age, locking her in an orphanage, and for making her believe she was my sister, knowing her, not only would she not speak to me anymore, but she would be able to make my nightmares come true: she could leave home and never go back, or do worse for how stubborn she is.

Many have tried to convince me to tell her the truth, from my father to Naily, who is forced to treat her as an ordinary child and not by her daughter.

And everyone continues to hate me, but I prefer to endure them and be seen by my daughter as a protective brother, rather than a father who didn't want to take on his responsibilities.

"See you tonight! It's almost lunchtime, but we are eating out.
»- my mother steals a kiss on the cheek, while I make a
grimace of contradiction.
"Where's Juliet?" - I ask in alarm, remembering how
much Clara wanted to see with a white dress on.
"She went out with a boy." - my mother shrugs, then slams the
door behind her:
«With whom?!» - I shout behind him, even if my mother cannot listen to me
and I cannot have an answer.

Nobody can touch my daughter, whether she wants it or not!
I hurry to get the keys and, without a shirt on, I walk swollen
towards the door, but as soon as I grab the handle someone
knocks insistently.

I frown and open the door to find myself in front of Andrew,
completely red in the face: «Do you want to break it ...?» -
before I can finish asking for explanations, he pushes me
inside the house and slams the door behind him again.
Only now do I notice that he is very pissed off, but I don't
have time to ask him what takes him: he raises an arm and
quickly punches me in the face:
«What the fuck ...» - I moan at the pain that that gesture
causes me, and then straighten my back again with the
palm of my hand on my cheekbone. I step back as he
steps forward to repeat the blow:
«What the fuck is it!» - I stop suddenly, remembering I have
Andrew in front of him, before he can split his face just for his
gesture.
"You said that you would leave Catherine as soon as you told
Juliet the truth!" - he says through his teeth, but he doesn't
give me time to calm him down, he continues:
"You fucked Catherine!" - she screams,
imitating me and pointing the index finger at my
forehead. Even more confused than before, I
tighten my jaw and take a grimace of disgust:

"What the fucking suck! No! "- I slap his hand to pull it away from my face:
«He looks like a blonde haired trans! Who put it in your head that I had sex with her? »- I close my eyes, and then start looking at him badly, not understanding why he believed such bullshit.

He frowns upset, then shakes the hand with which he hit me: he lowers his head and runs a hand through his hair in frustration, while he seems to get lost in thoughts.
"Do you have the cycle, by any chance?" - I add, taking on a painful grimace when I pass my hand on the point where he punched me and waiting for him to answer.

«Clara.» - he sighs, while every single muscle in my body contracts only upon hearing it named.
I lock myself in place and raise my chin to make him speak, now with a threatening expression:

«Do you know that Clara believes that you and Catherine ...?» - leaves the sentence in suspense, while I keep the same troubled expression as before.
«Fuck!» - I open my eyes, understanding what he means, while he looks at me attentively. «How can you think I brought her to bed!?» - I raise the volume of the voice again, seriously struck by Andrew's words.
«I don't know ... she was so sure.» - she says in a whisper, trying to calm me down, but I can't help shaking hands in two fists, going in search of something makes me crack on the ground to let off steam.

I love her so much that, fucking, even Chloe Kardashian, compared to her, seems to me a toilet!

I would never be able to look at a woman as I admire her, however childish and naive she may be at times, and even Tila Tequila with her ways would not be able to excite me, while Clara just has to bring a lock of hair behind her ear and blush to make me freak out.

«Here.» - as soon as he returns from the kitchen, Andrew hands me a cold beer, then takes a seat on the sofa and invites me to do the same.

"This explains why that day was so shocked." - he adds, as his words repeat themselves in my mind, finally making me understand Clara's strange behavior.
As an angry I slowly bend my lips upwards, then show my teeth and rest my elbows on my knees: I stare at the table in front of me, while silence falls.
But immediately afterwards I burst out laughing, turning to Andrew who looks at me confused, even if he raises an angle of his mouth upwards and tries to maintain a serious expression:
«Come on, jerk ... who knows how much he will have suffered.» - he says and tries not to smile, but I don't stop showing my teeth, laughing for the first time in such a long time.
"I thought she got tired of me." - I say again in a cheerful tone, to then add: "But she was jealous." - I shake my head, while I think how stupid I was for not having noticed.
I mentally retrace all the moments in which I saw her down and take on a serious expression, frowning:
"He must have suffered ..." - I repeat my friend's words to me, looking him in the eye: he nods in regret, making me understand that I have really hurt her, and I lose a beat at the mere thought that he may have cried for me.
"Why don't you talk to her?" - clears her throat, while I roll my eyes:

'That bitch told me to keep my mouth shut. And then ... Clara would feel guilty. »- I add with a whisper, while I bite my tongue so as not to start insulting Catherine unnecessarily.
"Do you think he would leave you not to hurt Juliet?" - I slowly nod to his question, then snort:
"Clara spoke of marriage." - he adds shortly after, as if he had just remembered it.
I nod, as I bring my lips upwards, smiling as I close my eyes and think about how beautiful she will be in a white dress. But she is beautiful regardless.
«I wanted it .» - I say with conviction, finally realizing how late I am: I quarreled with Clara about a stupid wedding, when, in reality, I have always seen her as my wife, from the first day I I met: from when we played gymkana, to when I hated her for going to study in Italy, to when she came back more beautiful than ever, to after having explored her whole body.

Clara is mine and I need a ring to mark my territory.

«You?!» - Andrew opens his eyes wide and starts to make fun of me, but I won't let him speak:

"I want to marry her in America, at my house, which Catherine doesn't know where she is. I want to make her mine and tell her the truth later, to convince her not to return to Australia, even if she is doing all this just to stay here. "
«And if
Catherine finds
out ?» - he asks
confusedly: «He
already knows .»
- I inform him ,
while he opens
his eyes:

"Like? And didn't you try to stop it? »- he insists, leaning forward.
«I sent her a message and I told her that I would abandon Clara on the altar.» - I nod to my words.
«So she accepted, because she thought this would have removed Clara from you definitively.» - continues in my place, while I raise my proud chin:
"You're a genius!" - he adds, but I avoid him, taking the phone in his hand and biting his lower lip:

* Alex and Catherine have entered your room. I tried to prevent it ... * - I type on the screen, pretending to be my daughter, and I send without thinking twice, then turn to Andrew: «You have to go!» - I say suddenly with a mischievous smile on my face, but my tone of voice disturbs him: «Why?» - he asks confused.
"Because Clara is coming."

C
h
a
p
t
e
r

4
2

"But where are you going!? You have your dress on! »- I let my mother scream from behind to walk swiftly towards John's car.
I keep my threatening expression and tighten my jaw, getting into the car, and, without even asking my friend's permission, I leave the parking lot.

The idea that they are about to stain my bed with their naked
bodies makes my blood boil in my veins and I stop thinking
just to treat them in the worst way.
I accelerate several times, despite having difficulty pressing
my foot against the accelerator, given the length of this dress.
If before I was thrilled by the idea of wearing it and I did everything
to not show that I was happy, now having it on does nothing but
annoy me and increase my desire to tear it away every second that
passes. I honk when a car slows down in front of mine, then
overtakes it impatiently.

I can't control the hatred I feel for Alex right now, especially for
not having had any mercy: he literally kicked me out of the
house with the excuse of the dress to be alone with Catherine,
but he could avoid taking her to the our bedroom.
Yet last night I held myself so tightly in my arms, as if he was
afraid of losing me, but only now I understand that he does not
fear this, in fact, he wants it.
I am frightened by the idea that behind all this mess there is a
plan formulated by him and Catherine to hurt me or make fun
of me, otherwise I will not explain how a second before you
can ask me to marry him and the one after having sex with his
real girlfriend, who even supported Alex's crazy idea. I'm really
afraid that the wedding day is not like my mother would expect
it, even if I will do everything to make sure that this day
doesn't come.

I explicitly forced Alex not to let Catherine come into my
house, but he seems to do it on purpose and does the
opposite of what I begged him not to do.
I grit my teeth, thinking about the worst ways to insult Catherine, even
at the cost of ruining everything: she could easily decide not to go
along with the wedding plan and tell my mother everything, but the
idea that this could happen doesn't scare me as much idea that right
now my blankets carry the scent of another woman.

I have often imagined, in spite of myself, Alex making Catherine feel the same pleasure she gives me, ending up crying every time, but now I will see them naked in front of my eyes, and at the mere thought of it I lose a beat.

I don't know how I would react, but I don't know, at that point, if I will have the courage to threaten them, rather than run away and let them continue.

I slow down the car in front of my garden, but without the anger that ran through my veins until recently.
I stare at the door from afar, terrified of what I could see beyond that, while I take a deep breath and pledge myself to fill the lungs with air at times.

I look down on the tulle of the dress to cover my legs and arms tight with elegant lace: I withdraw the tears, imagining my expression when I find them on my bed, I with a wedding dress on him, he with a blonde between arms...
My thoughts do not stop me from getting out of the car anyway, dragging behind the tail of the dress, while I join my hands and start fiddling with my thumbs, looking down and moving towards the entrance.

The wind hits my back, completely naked for the deep back neckline, while my collarbones emerge from the dress in the front: I cross my arms and shrug, then bring a lock of hair behind the ear and wait for it door opens by itself.
After a few moments of indecision I decide to put the key in the lock and go unconvinced, while finally my hair stops being moved by the wind.
I look around for a sign of Catherine's presence, but everything seems to be as I left it this morning, indeed, much more in order.
Silence reigns in the living room, so I decide to walk trembling towards my room. Approaching the door I begin to hear strange noises: I stop breathing when a moan runs away from Alex's mouth.

I immediately move away from the wood, holding a hand in front of my mouth and opening my eyes full of tears.
You are a heartless asshole!
The salty drops run down my cheekbones and I try with all my strength to grab the handle and enter to impress such a moment in the brain, but I lock myself in place, while I continue to stare at the dark wood, as if I could look through.
As soon as a sob escapes me, for fear of being discovered, I turn on my heels and go to leave with my heart in my throat, but at that exact moment the door opens and a laugh forces me to stop on the spot:
«I was joking, stop ...» - I turn again, even more amazed than before, but not as much as Alex, who opens his eyelids and swallows the saliva while looking at me from head to toe:
«Fuck ...» - she whispers in a choked voice, while I assume a confused expression, realizing that he is completely dressed.
I bite my tongue not to speak, then go to the door, pushing Alex to the side and looking inward.
The bed is completely redone and the blankets we fell asleep on remained on the ground, but above all there is no trace of that viper.

I quickly wipe away the tears, then return my attention to him, who still looks at me with a serious expression.
I glance at him from below, but this does not move him, on the contrary, he raises a corner of his mouth upwards, while he looks at me with tenderness, making a single dimple appear and making me feel embarrassed. I understand that he shamelessly lied to me and that it was he who sent me the message, making me run away from the atelier in a white suit.

He approaches, looking me straight in the eyes, while he cages my head with his gigantic hands, which rests behind my ears, and with his thumbs caresses my cheekbones.

I don't understand his intentions until he brings his lips close to my forehead to leave you a sweet kiss, one of those that I missed.
I feel curled up in his arms and I don't move to get away from there, although I should do it and slap him, for his stupid joke.

"Do you really think I can betray you?" - I snap my eyes to meet his.
His question leaves me perplexed: I frown at his words, analyzing them. «You ...» - I begin, but the words get stuck in my throat: «It was you who said it.» - I conclude with a whisper, but shakes his head slowly, getting closer and closer.
I keep my expression troubled as he tries to kiss me, but I take off and take two steps back: "What are you doing? Alex, you are engaged to Catherine! »- I try to make him reason with a

detached tone of voice: I don't understand why he made me come home, but I won't blind myself again to let him do my body what he wants.

«I've never had sex with her!» - she opens her arms, while I just close my eyes.
«But the messages said otherwise.» - I remember aloud, raising an eyebrow: he is really thinking he can make me believe otherwise, when I have all the tests and demonstrations to believe it.
"What did they say? That I fucked her? »- now he is taking on a grimace of disappointment. The messages I read on his phone did not explicitly express Alex's betrayal, but the meetings between him and Catherine.
I shake my head and return to reality, realizing how well he is confusing me.

«We've already talked about it, don't pretend !» - I cross my
arms under my chest, while Alex hurries to reply:
«No, instead! I thought like Andrew. "- he raises his voice,
while my heart starts pumping blood faster than usual -" That's
why you seemed like a spoiled child . "- she continues,
succeeding more and more in her intent.

He leans against the door frame with a frown on his face,
frowning, as if trying to remember the first times we fought
because of that viper.

"As a drunk you said you touched Catherine." - I start
talking again, but, for the umpteenth time, I am interrupted
by him, who raises his eyes to heaven and runs a hand
through his hair:

«I don't know what the fuck I said to you when I was drunk, I
don't remember it, but I didn't touch it.» - His conviction puts
me in crisis and my pupils dilate slowly:

«Catherine ...» - I try again, but she silences me, closing the
speech:

«Catherine just comes after me .» - I open my eyes
completely when I reach out and grab my wrist, then drag me
towards him and make me crash into his chest.

In the meantime he backs away and closes, with a quick gesture,
the door behind me, to then bring an arm under the skirt of this
dress and lift me up, while pushing my back against the cold
wood of the door.

«You don't know how much fucking I missed you.» -
stares at my lips, eager to fall on them, then I moisten
them with my tongue.

My gesture seems to make him lose patience, while my
trembling hand reaches the back of his neck, waiting for him
to press his mouth against mine, but he doesn't: he turns his

eyes on my face, almost wanting to check that every detail
of the my face was as it was the last time we were so close.

I let him touch every relief of the bones of my bare back with
his hand, while I pull his hair between my fingers, realizing
how superficial I was in believing Catherine's words.
As soon as his name comes to mind, I take a deep breath, bringing
my chest into contact with his.
I start to speak and stop him, slightly guilty, but he closes his
eyes and brings his head close to the hollow of my neck, sniffing
my skin, as if he wanted to appropriate my perfume, and then
calm me down, almost reading my mind:
«Don't think about it.» - he touches the back of my ear with the tip of his
nose, while his sigh is spreading on my neck and I don't find the
courage to breathe, if not to close my eyes, while he continues:
«I want to enjoy you.» - he whispers on my shoulder, making
me shiver for his hungry tone.

C
h
a
p
t
e
r

4
3

I let him caress my arm as he returns to look me in the eyes,
making me lose a beat. He finally brings attention to my lips,
but he doesn't seem to want to make the first move to make
me impatient: I would not want to give him the chance to win,
but his mouth is so inviting that I bring the tip of my nose close
to his, and then stick to his lips and invite him to make me feel
his taste, urging the corner of his mouth with the tip of his

tongue, the same one that immediately afterwards lifts him mischievously.

He is not slow to be satisfied and fill my mouth with his tongue: I frown, moaning for having noticed only now how much I missed.
I squeeze his hair in my hands for pleasure, but my gesture seems to excite him, in fact he sighs heavily against my nostrils.

He pulls me away from the door, then searches for the zip of the dress, while he leaves me standing on the floor. I help him quickly, but then he forces me to put my hands on his already messy hair, while slowly he lowers the dress, without stopping to look at me.
My skin is completely exposed to his eyes, and he seems to pay no attention to my belly, which makes me believe John's words.
Maybe Alex is not only justifying himself, maybe he really is telling the truth, but even if he was lying to me, at this moment I would never find the courage to go back.
I keep lying to myself that one day I will be able to forget him and move on without him, but the truth is that I am addicted to Alex.
I loved to go crazy even when I thought I had been betrayed by him and I let him go in Catherine's arms, without speaking clearly with Alex.
I misunderstood everything and I planted myself only because of my impulsiveness, but in the end it has always been so with him.
When it comes to Alex I stop thinking and immediately think of the worst: I insulted him, avoided and blamed him for something he never did!
I shouldn't have believed Catherine and I shouldn't have believed him drunk.
«Wait ...» - my thoughts have the upper hand again and the doubts come back to haunt me, as he raises his arms to take off his shirt.

I forget the question I was going to ask him, while
my eyes light up as I stare at the familiar black
ink that goes up to his neck. «What?» - he
whispers in a hoarse voice.

Only on seeing him so hungry, my chest goes up and down
and I can't breathe enough oxygen because of his hands that
come back to rest under my back: I tie my legs around his
pelvis, while my intimacy collides with the hardness of your
abs.
Raise your chin, waiting for an answer from me, but I can't
help biting my lower lip and whispering:
«I love you .» - to then see him show off both dimples on the
sides of his mouth.
«I know.» - he says with pride, while I continue to fix a dimple:
I can't resist again and I give a quick kiss right in that point of
the cheek, making his smile widen.
I sling over his mouth, without letting him say anything else,
and then push the pelvis slightly against his bare skin: he
twists his lips around mine as only he can do, as he walks
towards the bed. Tilt your torso, making my back adhere
gently to the mattress and position yourself between my legs,
which widens to make room and lower its intimacy on mine,
while its mouth does not stop leaving wet trails along my neck:

«Not everyone has understood that you are mine ...» - he says
in a hoarse and low tone, but I can't find the strength to lower
my head to meet his eyes, while he moves his lips against my
collarbone: I understand the meaning of his words when I feel
his teeth gently grasp my skin, which leads me to leave a
silent moan, choked by the sound that comes out of his mouth
when, involuntarily, I sink my nails into the muscles of his arm.

«My mother and Clelia might notice it.» - I use what little
lucidity I have left to try to convince him:
"To hell with it!" - continues to bite me, kiss me and make me
touch the sky with a finger for simple kisses on the neck, but I
realize that I have not yet felt anything when it comes down to
the space between the breasts. I blush from head to toe and a
strong desire in my belly makes my arch arch, unwittingly
approaching my chest to his lips.

He looks up to look at me, almost wanting to memorize the
way I enjoy thanks to him for a little touch on his part.
He reaches the bra with two fingers and, without taking it off,
pushes his hand under his underwear, gently caressing me: I
feel so dirty, but at the same time clean and naive under his
attentive gaze. I pass my hand from his biceps to his hair,
which start to tickle my belly, while Alex continues to torture
me, biting my skin as if in this way he could get hold of it, even
if he is already aware that I belong to him and nobody else.

I open my mouth, but I hurry to take the lower lip between my
teeth so as not to moan loudly, when I feel the upper part of my
intimacy, still barely covered, being kissed by her mouth: I leave
her hair and go looking for something to hold between your
fingers so as not to scream with pleasure, so I'm satisfied with a
piece of blanket that I twist in a fist.

«Alex ...» - my choked voice almost seems to implore
him not to continue to torture me and immediately
leave his mark on my intimacy.
«What do you want?» - he asks in a tone so seductive that I
could be satisfied to come under his clever eyes: he looks at
me without malice, indeed, almost with tenderness, while he
raises the right corner of his mouth and stares at me, then
grabs the underpants, in the part that covers my sex, between
the index and middle fingers and slowly pull the underwear
down my thighs.

I am completely naked and drunk under her arms, which I
promised myself would never happen again.

I didn't keep my promise, but it was worth it ...

«Kiss me, please!» - I beg him , while his eyes light up and,
without thinking twice, he lowers his eyes, looking at me.

I prepare to shout his name when I feel the warmth of his
tongue pass through me: my moans are followed by his,
while I flex my legs for pleasure.

I moan for every single day I have spent without him and
abandon myself to Alex for all the times I have thought of him
as a ruthless traitor.
In one day Alex went from being the man of my nightmares to my
man: I hated and loved him again, several times since the day he
started attracting my attention, but I never loved him as I love him
now, as he enters me with quick but delicate movements, as if he
knew of the existence of the twins and feared to hurt them.

I love him the moment he makes me come, helping me to empty
myself of all the evil that I had to endure because of Catherine,
because now I have the certainty that he will never have eyes
for her, but only for me, regardless of my large sweatshirts and
disgusting, from Catherine's perfect body, and the little
experience I have in bed.

He loves me, even if he doesn't reproach him often, and it is
enough for me to be able to forget his vices and the two months
of torture that I spent, because Alex has become a damned
medicine.

I didn't remember Alex's torso so hard on contact with my skin, while his arm surrounds my chest and draws me to him, squeezing my breasts between my muscles.
«You went under with boxing.» - I let him embrace me, while his body gives off heat under the already heavy blankets.
«Just for you.» - I can imagine her amused expression, but I don't turn to her side and close my eyes when she leaves a kiss in my hair.

We have so many things to say, yet we are talking about his perfect body: I have many questions to ask him and Alex owes me answers, but neither of us wants to ruin a heavenly moment like this.

It seems to me centuries have passed since the last time we fell asleep on the same bed, but now we are finally alone: there is only me, Alex and the twins, in our house.
I put my lower lip between my teeth and hold back a smile, getting as close to him as possible to be pampered like a child.
I return to feeling protected by him as in the old days, when I liked the idea of being childish and inexperienced, because only in this way could he see me as his little girl.

Happier than ever, I move from my seat and lean my torso forward to grab Alex's sweatshirt, even if involuntarily I bring my back to his intimacy, and then hear him sigh heavily:

«I don't mind shooting again.» - he laughs, making me blush,
then imitating me and approaching my back with my lips.
Chills come back to dominate my spine when it bites a point in
my shoulder blade, making me suddenly scream:
«Alex!» - I turn to her side, laughing close to her lips, then
leave us a quick kiss and walk away again, with her shirt
still in her hand and now kneeling on the bed.

He gets up on the bed, until he surpasses me in height, to then
grab me by the elbow and push me towards him, while he lets
himself fall from the opposite side of the bed: I find myself with
the elbows on his chest and my naked intimacy on his leg.

«I love you too.» - he says suddenly, placing the palm of his
hand on the lower part of my back, and then he begins to
draw imaginary circles with his thumb.

He says those words in a way so natural and unexpected that
my heartbeat increases wildly, while I put both hands on the
sides of his neck, stained by the black ink very familiar to me.
«Really?» - I whisper, continuing to look him in the eyes, as if I
wanted to be sure, for his part, of something that I am sure of
regardless.

He frowns and takes a frown, almost offended by my words:
"Why do you ask?" - he seems really impressed by my question, which
leads me to regret having reacted in that way.

«Why ...» - I try to find the right words to express what I think without
hurting him: I have doubted several times about his feelings towards
me, but only because sometimes he seems to get away from me and
forget about my existence.

But now I understand that Alex has his own way to show that he
cares about me: every time we fight, his eyes change color,
becoming darker; when I tell him to go out with a being who is
not a woman, he asks me for life, death and miracles to make
sure that he is only an old man with prostatitis, and for work

reasons only, otherwise he becomes jealous and goes crazy; he agrees to take a step forward in our relationship only when he thinks he is risking losing me.

In fact, we had to argue about the wedding, but he suddenly showed himself ready to marry me when he realized that otherwise I would have gone away from him.

He is not the threatening man, all muscles and tattoos, with me, but a weak man who is afraid of losing me and capable of anything in order to make sure that I belong to none other than him.

«Why don't you tell me often.» - I shrug my shoulders, trying not to make a tragedy of it, and I lower my eyes, but with the other hand I raise my chin and force me to meet his sweetened gaze:
«Look at me.» - his looks like a prayer, rather than an order, and I can't help doing as he says, eagerly waiting for me to say what I would like to hear coming from his lips.
«I don't tell you often ...» - he says raising his chin and confirming my words, and then continuing - «... and I would like you to do it too.» This time I am taking on a confused expression:
"Shouldn't I tell you I'm in love with you?" - I frown , not understanding where he wants to go, while he nods.
«Why?» - I insist, since it seems so absurd to me: a normal copy exchanges demonstrations of affection, and that's what I expected from my relationship with Alex, even if he is not like other men. He runs his tongue between his lips, distracting me for a thousandth of a second, and then helping me to interpret his words.

«It seems you want to remind me.» - his words make me narrow my eyes and lift the corners of my mouth upwards:
«But we both know we are fucked.» - he imitates me smiling, while his eyes end up on the my mouth, which approaches his with a quick gesture, surrounding my head with one arm, then pushing it down.

He sucks my lips, filling the room with a beautiful noise,
but immediately afterwards I move away and hurry to put
on my sweatshirt, shivering with the cold of the last hours
of the afternoon. She complains, while I enjoy the taste of
Alex left on my mouth, undecided whether to start talking
about the topic that neither of them wants to open or not.
Out of the corner of my eye I observe every detail of his body,
almost to make sure that everything is as I remembered, but I
notice that it has changed very quickly, as I had already
perceived from the moment when my bare skin touched his.
When I drag my eyes to her intimacy I feel my cheeks go up in
flames:
«You continue to blush even if you are familiar.» - he
brings his hands behind the back of his neck, while he
gives me a wink.

I avoid her gaze, even more embarrassed than before,
and then put my feet on the ground. I shiver again,
realizing that I have bare legs, even if covered to the top
of the knees by the sweatshirt fabric.
"Er ..." - clears his throat, almost about to speak, as I
approach the wardrobe and open a door wide.
«Don't take it off.» - indicates the sweatshirt I wear with my
chin: «I like it when you put on my shirts.» - he confesses for
the first time after the countless times he has seen me do the
same.

«I wouldn't have done it.» - I say with a sure tone and I bring a
lock of hair behind my ear, while he raises a corner of his
mouth, X-raying me when I tiptoe up and raise my arms,
discovering his thighs before his penetrating gaze.

«You have become skeletal.» - she starts talking again, but this time with a severe tone, but at her words I burst out laughing.
I eat worse than Molly in Mike & Molly because of the grapes that I find inside my belly, and being told that I have lost weight can only make me laugh in the face of those who tell me, in this case Alex.

He raises an eyebrow and maintains a serious expression, which makes me stop showing my teeth and imitating his seriousness:
"Really?"
He does not respond and continues to look at me from head to toe, while I imitate him, although I do not seem to notice any change.
"You don't eat, do you? You keep doing those fucking anorexic diets ... »- the tone of his voice is defensive, even if he seems angry at the moment.
I roll my eyes, undecided whether to believe him or not, but finally I decide to avoid him and go back to look for a pair of clean underwear.
«I eat more than you.» - I reassure him after a while, without looking him in the eyes, but I can't help but jump for joy mentally: for years I have been trying to impress him and lose weight to appear attractive to his eyes, but apparently I only managed it now.
«Sure.» - he says ironically, therefore, without thinking twice, I open my mouth:
"Yes but! Two hours ago Luois offered me a slice of ... »- my enthusiasm diminishes when I realize what I just missed.
I'm stupid!
I narrow my eyes, not having the courage to face his anger after such an intense afternoon. «Alex ...» - I whisper when I notice that silence falls in the room: I only pronounce his name, but I also implore him implicitly not to get out of my mind and wait for an explanation from me.

Only after other moments of silence do I find the courage to open my eyes, to find him staring at me with my jaw set and my eyes slightly red with anger.

That expression says more than a thousand words, and bad words, for Alex, and it is enough for me to understand that he is seriously angry: I shouldn't have opened my mouth and I feel terribly guilty for going out with Louis, even knowing that Alex would not have done pleasure. After all, I was angry with him and maybe it was a kind of revenge on my part, but now I can't help but repent.

His eyes are terribly threatening and they seem to want to ask me for more details, while he clearly holds back and tries not to burst with fury, which I can still read in his contracted muscles.

Continue not to speak, while it seems to formulate a sentence with full meaning, which does not contain any swear words or blasphemy:

"Swear to me that he hasn't touched you these days." - the tone of his voice is so cold that I lose a beat and I feel the blood freeze in my veins, while the kiss between me and Louis immediately comes to mind.

C
h
a
p
t
e
r

4
5

His words are repeated in my head several times, while he waits for an answer.

I do not have the courage to tell him the truth, fearing that I will have an angry man in front of me again. It was all so magical, from the

moment he told me the truth to the way he made me feel so far and I don't want to go back in time, but my silence is already being interpreted by Alex: «I understand.» - his sharp voice is worse than a punch in the stomach, so I can't help but lie:
"No, no! He didn't touch me . »- I hurry to shake my head, showing myself as determined as possible, even if I can't look him in the eyes, but then I sigh and quickly approach his body, positioning myself astride his abdominals.
I bring my chest forward and rest my lips on his to try to calm him:
"He's just a friend." - I take my eyes off his as he continues to stare at me with clenched teeth:
"Don't look at me like that, please." - I beg him to stop torturing me.
«Alternatively I can go and split his face.» - he is serious while expressing his anger and I understand that it is better to change the subject, rather than increase his anger:
«I should be the angry one .» - I say, but my words are not only an excuse to calm him: I too am a victim in this situation, since he tortured me for weeks just to make me jealous. «You owe me a bit of explanation.» - I rest my elbows on her tattoos, while I harden my gaze: «Does Catherine know you only love me?» - I don't know why absurd reason I feel almost guilty for her: Alex he used it for a selfish purpose.

His expression changes from threatening to amused, as he looks at me from below: "No." - he limits himself, shrugging his shoulders as if nothing had happened.
"Tell him, then!" - I do n't think twice before exclaiming:
«I don't know, I was starting to like you as a girlfriend.» - he raises a corner of his mouth at the top and looks at me attentively, while the smile dies on my lips.
«Ah yes?» - I raise an eyebrow, while he widens his smile widens.
I understand the playful tone of his voice, so I slowly approach his wide neck: «So some did not

understand that you are mine.» - I whisper, imitating
his own tone of voice, while a light laugh escapes
him.
I claim the pacifier which is now clearly visible at the base of
my neck, fortunately in a place where I can easily hide it.
«Mmm ...» - gasps in my hair, while I slide my fingers on his
chest, retracing his reliefs, to then reach the triangle, while his
muscles contract under my hand. «Fuck ...» - she whispers,
bringing her hand through my already messy hair.
I try to reach his wet intimacy with the palm of my hand, but I
jerk and lift my head when I hear the thud of the door, a sign
of the fact that it has been opened:
"Clara, are you at home?" Clelia's voice makes my eyes widen and,
without realizing it, I press my hand against her intimacy.
«Ah ...» - a groan runs away, while he tries to hold back a
laugh.
My grimace of embarrassment remains, as I jump up from his
body, to immediately put on the first pair of pants that I find in the
closet, completely forgetting my underwear.

«Pretend nothing!» - I turn to his side, but I still find him
relaxed, while he looks at me with a frown, but at the same
time amused by my gestures:
«But really?» - she points her fingers down and only now do I
notice the pole between her legs: I immediately look away, as
if it were the first time I realized how big it is.

I mentally slap myself to be able to think about Alex's genital,
while my mother-in-law looks for me two meters away.
«Hide it!» - I refrain from shouting at it in a loud voice, almost
envious of its serenity, while I try to make myself presentable
in two seconds, and then go towards the living room, but not
before I have lifted the wedding dress from the floor.

«There is no one in the house.» - my mother mumbles,
turned away, but Clelia notices me, then raises her chin in
surprise and starts to open her mouth, but I interrupt her
and raise my hands, which grasp the bust of the dress,
This can be noted:
"It's the right one ." - I nod to my words, immediately thinking
of the answers to be given to my mother's questions.
Clelia smiles and sighs, as if she had deprived herself of a
weight, while the other brings her eyes to the ceiling. "Thank
goodness, because we have already paid." - I lower my head,
slightly sorry, but at the same time I am struck by many different
emotions.

I have never felt so happy, especially after knowing that
Alex has never betrayed me, but also for calming my thirst:
I was thirsty for him and his kisses.
I see with different eyes even my mother and Clelia, whom I
can finally return to call 'motherin-law': thanks to them I am
going to marry the man I love.

I'm getting married ...
At the mere thought that my wishes are coming true and that
my life is going from a nightmare to a bomb of emotions, I
doubt that all this is true and I start to fear that it is a dream
and that's it, that tomorrow I will wake up with tears in his
eyes, aware that Alex will never be mine and that the marriage
is only the result of a plan.

But, if it were a dream, my mother would be much kinder
and more enthusiastic, and surely would not ask me for
explanations:
"You made us take a hit." - Clelia tilts her head with a frown,
but then it's my mother who takes the floor:
"Why did you run away like that?"
She takes me unprepared, but now I have become an expert
liar and I have the excuse ready: I have not yet told Alex that I
am pregnant, wanting to make sure that he has not lied to me
again, I told him that I have not kissed Louis, already imagining

his reaction when he finds out, and now I'm shamelessly lying to my mother:

«I wanted Alex to see him on me .» - the trembling voice betrays me, while Alex supports me only with a pair of pants on, but with a naked torso.

«On you, or at your feet?» - my mother asks ironically to herself, but does not hide a small mischievous smile.

I blush violently, even though she's right and it is clear that Alex and I are not innocent: «Mom?!» - I glance quickly at Clelia, who seems to be ashamed as I am, while I think about how to tell my mother to stop put myself in such situations, without offending her, even if sometimes it seems to me that she does it on purpose.

"You could take a picture and send it to him." - shrugs, as if he hadn't said anything exaggerated. I do not have time to reply that he starts talking again, without calculating himself in the least, while I would like to shout to the man at my side to put on a shirt.

«We will cook tonight. You can go back to show Alex the dress . »- finally meets my gaze, but now in vain, so I put a hand in my hair and roll my eyes.

I remain silent as a sign of acceptance, as I cross my arms over my chest, watching her walk towards the kitchen with Clelia.

If only she learned to be more serious, she would really do me a great favor, sparing me the foolish things that I continue to do because of her.

But now I gave up and got used to it, so I let off steam with Alex, who looks at me with a frown, rather than amused, as I expected:

"You could have covered yourself!" - I take him back, pulling him a light slap on the bare chest. «We are getting married.» -

shrugs, then resumes talking after moments of silence: «What should we do? Dancing the tango? »- I shake my head at his words, only now realizing how similar my mother and Alex are to their brazenness.
"But did it cost you so much to look for a shirt?" - I ask between my teeth, still with my arms crossed under my chest, while a confused expression appears again on his face:
"It's what I was doing, but ..." - he stops, almost trying to think of how to formulate a question, and then concludes:

"Why are there baby clothes in our closet?"

End of SECOND part

Author: Ema Oqu

Instagram: ema_8579

Facebook Ema Oqu